WINTER'S WALTZ

THE WICKED WINTERS BOOK 11

SCARLETT SCOTT

HAPPILY EVER AFTER BOOKS

Winter's Waltz
The Wicked Winters Book 11

All rights reserved.

Copyright © 2021 by Scarlett Scott

Published by Happily Ever After Books, LLC

Edited by Grace Bradley

Cover Design by Wicked Smart Designs

This book or any portion thereof may not be reproduced or used in any manner whatsoever without the express written permission of the publisher except for the use of brief quotations in a book review.

The unauthorized reproduction or distribution of this copyrighted work is illegal. No part of this book may be scanned, uploaded, or distributed via the Internet or any other means, electronic or print, without the publisher's permission. Criminal copyright infringement, including infringement without monetary gain, is punishable by law.

This book is a work of fiction and any resemblance to persons, living or dead, or places, events, or locales, is purely coincidental. The characters are productions of the author's imagination and used fictitiously.

For more information, contact author Scarlett Scott.

www.scarlettscottauthor.com

❦ Created with Vellum

In memory of Monique Daoust

CHAPTER 1

LONDON, FEBRUARY 1815

The Marquess of Sundenbury was not going to last more than ten minutes in the East End. Genevieve Winter was never more certain of it than when she found him seated in *her* chair at *her* desk at Lady Fortune, his polished boots propped upon *her* ledgers, grinning like the stupid, handsome fiend he was.

He was not going to last because she was going to murder him.

Poison, she decided. He was too pretty to suffer the agony of gunshot or the blade. Mayhap she could slip hemlock into his tea.

"Miss Winter," he said, not bothering to rise.

The omission suited her perfectly fine, she told herself. Gen did not prefer to be treated as a lady. She wore breeches, shirt, cravat, and boots this morning. It was ever so much more comfortable than stays and gowns. Why did chaps get to claim the best garments for themselves?

"What the hell are you doing in my office, you spoony twat?" she demanded.

He winced, as if her vulgar words caused him physical pain. Gen hoped they did.

"Is that any way to greet the man who will be your companion—indeed, your saving grace—for the next month?"

"Saving grace?" She snorted, crossing her arms over her chest and pinning him with a glare. "Pain in my arse, more like."

What the devil had she been thinking when she had agreed to this bloody addlepated idea of her half brothers' wives? Lady Addy and Lady Evie, twins who were married to her half brothers Dom and Devil, had suggested the plan to her after their brother's last embarrassment.

Having been banished from The Devil's Spawn thanks to his inability to control his gambling, he had somehow wormed his way into the rival gaming hell owned by the Suttons. And he had promptly gotten tap-hackled and lost ten thousand pounds.

He had also had his purse strings cut by his father the duke.

Fitting, in her opinion. The old duke ought to have boxed his ears and sent him to Elba with Boney while he was at it.

Sundenbury quirked a brow at her, and then the blighter lifted a cigar to his lips, giving it a puff and sending a cloud of smoke in her direction. "You have a fine arse, Miss Winter. I would hate to cause it any pain."

He sounded so polite, with those crisp, aristocratic accents of his. And yet he looked thoroughly dissolute. His cravat was undone, and he was down to his shirtsleeves. His wavy, dark hair was ruffled, as if some obliging wench had recently run her fingers through it.

She probably had. Gen would make her next order of business a trip to the ladies employed by The Devil's Spawn. Her unwanted charge was not to be cozying up with lady-

For making her skin go hot and feel too tight for her body.

Lust, she told herself. It was what she had felt for Gregory, curse his rotten hide. A weakness. Proof she was made of flesh and bone, a reminder from above that she was mortal.

Imperfect.

She sneered. "You don't want my worst, yournabs."

She was speaking flash, when she had been studying so damned carefully to keep her vulgar tongue at bay. That was what this man's presence in her sphere—her own gaming hell, which she had worked her fingers to the bone securing —did to her.

Intolerable.

Unacceptable.

There were other words—bigger words, the words of a lady, taught to her by her half sisters-in-law, but she had forgotten them. The first two would do.

He was smiling again, that knowing scoundrel's grin that probably made all the ladies swoon and fetch their smelling salts. Grinning, actually. And the man had dimples. Two dents in his cheeks which ought to have been annoying but were, in fact, alluring.

Rather than hindering his looks, those two unlikely divots heightened them. All the more reason to dislike the man. And his face. Especially his mouth. Those bloody dimples, too.

"I assure you, Miss Winter—Genevieve. I can weather your worst." The scoundrel dared to touch her then. He dragged the knuckles of his right hand along her jaw in a silken caress that made shivers dance up and down her spine. "It is more than apparent you do not want me here. I can alleviate your frustrations. For the right price, I will go."

She clenched her jaw and slapped his hand away from her face. "Are you suggesting I *pay* you?"

The man had worms for brains. This was a terrible idea. What could he possibly teach her about polishing her mannerisms? A carriage wreck was what he was. A *scourge*. Aye, rats were in his larder. He was an utter disaster.

A handsome disaster, but a disaster nonetheless. And one who thought he could charm himself out of his obligation.

"I am, admittedly, pockets to let at the moment," he said, with a rather sheepish air, as if he had done nothing at all to land himself in his current predicament.

His intolerable masculine scent—something tangy and sharp and altogether pleasing in the fashion of a fancy gentleman who gave a shite about the way he looked and smelled—only made matters worse.

"I ain't paying you," she growled. "And you are standing too close to me. Move."

He did not retreat, but he did move. Those bloody fingers of his were back on her jaw, then down her neck, tracing to her cravat. "Your pulse suggests you do not mind, pet."

He had received his final warnings. And yet he dared to remain where he was, crowding her with his larger body, touching her, and calling her *pet*. There was only one answer she could give.

Gen's brother Gavin was a prizefighter, and he had taught her, in painstaking detail, how to defend herself. Forming a fist in the proper fashion—thumb tucked against the knuckles of her forefinger and middle finger—she took aim and landed her blow squarely upon its intended target.

The Marquess of Sundenbury's aristocratic nose.

* * *

THE HELLION HAD *PUNCHED* HIM.

Right in the damned nose.

Max held his hand over the wounded appendage, which was throbbing, and he hoped *not* broken. His eyes were watering—not tears, curse it all—and he could not have been more shocked. Oh, Miss Genevieve Winter had threatened to break his fingers and his nose. But she was a *woman*. No member of the fairer sex in his acquaintance had ever physically attacked a man. An outraged mistress tossing about vases and the occasional slipper or curio—hell, even a mantel clock—was perfectly understandable. A female landing a fist to a man's nose, however, not so much.

Then again, she was a woman ostensibly garbed as a male, from her perfectly knotted cravat to her polished boots, which were far too small to belong to a man. She must have commissioned them for her measurements. He had taken note at the same time he had admired the manner in which her trousers clung to her limbs and the delightful—if slight—swell of her hips. Ordinarily, Max preferred a more voluptuous sort of female. However, there was no denying that Miss Genevieve Winter's willowy form was as sultry as any well-endowed woman he had ever known. He would gladly bed her in the next breath if she seemed inclined.

And if he could get his dratted nose to cease aching. *Christ*, his fingers were slick with warm liquid, which could only be—

"Is your nose bleeding?" she asked calmly, as if she were not the reason for his current agony.

He released his nose long enough to hold his hand before him and confirm, before fishing a handkerchief from his waistcoat and pressing it to his nostrils to stop the flow. "Yes, it is."

Although he attempted to glare at the delectable creature who had just punched him in the nose, he was not certain his attempts at sternness could be appreciated in his current state. Meanwhile, she was perched on the edge of her desk, those beautiful legs of hers dangling, sinfully outlined in her trousers.

He entertained a brief fantasy of those limbs wrapped around his waist as he plunged deep inside her before reason chased it.

"It may be broken," she observed, crossing her legs and flattening her palms on the ledgers-and-correspondence-laden surface of her desk.

As if she had not a care.

And blast her, but he could not tear his gaze from those curvaceous limbs of hers even as he attempted to sop up the blood streaming from his right nostril. Only the right, it seemed. A promising sign? One could only hope. He had been planted a facer before, naturally. However, everyone before her had been kind enough to avoid his nose and aim instead for his jaw.

"I am certain it is unbroken," he argued stubbornly, for this scrap of a female was *not* going to outdo him.

Oh no. Not today, Satan's minion.

He had formulated his plan quite carefully. He would relieve himself of this most unwanted duty and carry on with his life. His father would forgive him for his sins, in time. This latest, regrettable scrape would fade into obscurity where it belonged. After all, the duke could cut the purse strings but he could not sever the familial ties. The heir was the heir, and the heir was...Max.

Such as he was.

Currently, stranded in an East End gambling den with a siren dressed in gentleman's garb who had just landed a deuced smarting blow to his nose. He had thought he could charm her and avoid her. Clearly, he would have to concoct a new strategy.

"It is bleeding rather profusely," she pointed out, with an arched, golden brow.

Not to mention nary a hint of contrition.

"Fancy word for an East End lady," he grumbled from behind his blood-stained handkerchief. *"Profusely."*

Small of him, he knew.

But the damned woman had wounded him—and doubly so. No female he had ever met had *struck* him. Or denied him, for that matter.

She hopped down from the desk in spritely fashion. "I was about to fetch you some ice to help staunch the flow, but now you are decidedly on your own, Blunderberry."

She had ice here? The establishment was not nearly as ramshackle as he had supposed prior to his arrival, but it hardly looked as if she would have spare ice waiting about. And surely his ears were mistaken and she had not just referred to him as—

"Suiting name, no?" She grinned, unapologetic, both for the damage she had done his poor nose and the insult she had paid his title.

An honorific was still a goddamn honorific, which was far more than this bastard, rookeries-born spawn of a cit— clad in a gentleman's attire—could ever hope for. He ought to spank her arse for the outrage.

Bloody wonderful.

Now his cock was throbbing in tandem with his beak.

And he had also just thought of his nose as a goddamn *beak*. Her word. Next, he would be saying spoony. *Good God*, what a horror. The word ought to be outlawed. *Damnation*. Was it even a word?

"Hardly suiting, Miss Winter."

How nettling that his voice was rendered somewhat nasally by the necessity of pressing his handkerchief over the bleeding appendage which would not be named.

"You may call me Gen." She cocked her head at him, eying him with a sweeping glance that went from head to toe. "Everyone does. Enemies included."

She considered him an enemy, then? Intriguing. He could use that in his favor. Most of the ladies in his acquaintance were thoroughly charmed by his looks, his wit, and most especially by his future as the next Duke of Linross.

This one was different.

Not merely because of her...*interesting* form of dress. Downright distracting, that. Little wonder it was not polite for ladies to gad about in anything other than gowns. The delineation of her legs was maddening. Even with a bleeding, smarting nose.

Of which she was the source, he reminded himself, gritting his teeth.

"Miss Winter shall do fine," he countered. If she thought to make him dance to her bidding, she was wrong.

Never mind that he had nary a ha'penny to his name at the moment. Or that he was rather at this woman's mercy thanks to the intervention of his sisters. Fortunately, he loved Evie and Addy, else he would have never agreed to this abomination. Then again, begging their heartless father's mercy seemed a rather cold and unwanted option at the moment. Max's former mistress would not harbor him without the coin and gifts he had once lavished upon her—all gone thanks to his latest bout of terrible luck.

The turn of fortune's wheel had never benefitted him, it was true. Never had there been greater evidence of that sad fact than now. And fitting, in a bitter sense, that he found himself in a nascent gaming hell christened Lady Fortune.

Lady Fortune was a bloody witch. So, he was becoming increasingly convinced, was this establishment's owner.

"Gen," she countered, "or I'll have you tossed out on your arse."

There had been a rather large and imposing fellow haunting the front hall—all muscle, menacing as a goddamn lion. Had an inking of a skull on his neck. Max did not think he would like to trespass on the wrong side of that man's magnanimity. Still, if he expected to gain anything from this farce, he needed the stubborn female before him to understand he would not kowtow to her or any of her lackeys.

He quirked a brow—not an easy feat considering his nose still hurt like a bastard. "You haven't the strength to toss me out on my arse, pet."

Those beautiful blue eyes of hers snapped with fire.

Her pretty pink lips thinned. "I warned you about calling me pet. Try me again, Blunderberry. I won't give a toss about sending Peter in to collect your sorry bones."

Peter. That was the beast's name? Hardly seemed fitting.

He wondered just how close Miss Gen Winter was to this Peter with the skull-bedecked neck. And then he wondered why he gave a damn.

Stupid.

He had not suffered the degradation of showing his face at this deuced establishment so he could lust over its most unusual proprietress.

Speaking of which…

Max pinned Miss Gen Winter beneath his most ducal glare. Admittedly, the effect was likely hindered by the necessity of holding the besmirched handkerchief to his bleeding —and possibly broken—nose. "If you do me more harm, or have any of your lackeys injure me, you will not have your lessons in becoming a lady, will you? Indeed, if you intend to insult and abuse me, consider yourself no longer in possession of my aid, Miss Winter."

There. He sounded confident. Like a man who could afford to be rude to the lady he was being forced to instruct in etiquette for the next damned month.

Ha! Quelle *lark*.

"Hate to say it, Blunderberry, but you aren't about to slip me the Dublin packet. You owe my family."

How lovely. Miss Gen Winter was aware of his reduced circumstances in every way. He had been hoping the damned Winters—particularly Mr. Dominic Winter, his sister Addy's husband and general East End Croesus—would have granted him some dignity and neglected to inform their sister of the debts which had been settled on his behalf.

Apparently not.

"Nevertheless," he bit out, taking away the damned handkerchief at last, "if you are not amenable to the task, I shall be more than happy to find another means of satisfying my debts."

She had the audacity to laugh at him. "Just as you have satisfied all your other debts, Blunderberry? I think not. This is the only way we'll be getting what is owed, and I intend to collect."

Blast.

He scowled at her and then grimaced, because scowling bloody well hurt, curse the woman. "Consider this our first lesson, Miss Winter. Ladies do not strike gentlemen."

"Eh." She raised a brow and crossed her arms over her waistcoat, drawing his attention to the slight swells of her breasts hidden beneath. "You don't look much like a gentleman, Blunderberry."

This chit was going to be the death of him before the month was over. Max was predicting it now.

His scowl turned into a glare. Moderately less painful than the scowl had been. "Touché, Miss Winter. You do not look much like a lady from where I stand either."

She sauntered toward him, exuding a confidence that was rare amongst females—unless they were courtesans, of course—drawing to a halt within kissing distance. "Here's the way of it, *yournabs*. I don't want to be a bloody lady. I just want to know how one thinks and acts so I can persuade as many of them as possible to come to Lady Fortune and give me their blunt."

There was honesty, he supposed. And he could not help but to think of himself in those same terms. To wonder if that was how every gaming hell proprietor thought about him and other noble clientele.

Max leaned down until their noses almost brushed. Until her breath skated over his lips, tea-scented and alluring. Of course. He took a moment to appreciate the unusual beauty of her features. She did not possess an ordinary loveliness— not the fragile beauty expected from a diamond of the first water. But she was exquisite in her individuality, in the ferocity she exuded, in the disparity she represented. Flaxen hair, icy eyes, rosebud lips, the slashes of her cheeks, the strength of her brows, the prominence of her jaw, the gentleman's attire, the spare form.

Rare.

That was what she was.

And maddening, too.

But never mind all that now. He had a far more pressing concern.

"If you want me to help you empty the reticules of every gambling-minded lady in London," he told her, "then you had damned well better refrain from punching me in the nose in future, madam."

She sniffed. "You earned that one, Blunderberry. Don't dare to suggest you didn't."

With that, she turned on her heel and sauntered away. He would be a liar if he said he was not watching the sway of her hips in those damned trousers of hers.

He was watching.

And she was exquisite.

Or mayhap her bottom was?

Both, he decided. Her rump and all the rest of her, too.

"Stop ogling my arse," she commanded, as if she knew what he was about.

And then she rang the bell pull.

In the next few seconds, the dreaded Peter appeared.

CHAPTER 2

Gen jolted awake at dawn to the certainty of a presence in her chamber. She was in bed, the counterpane to her chin. She did not stretch. Did not rise. Took care to maintain the even breaths of sleep, to keep from alerting the interloper that she was awake.

Danger was nothing new to her. She had cut her teeth in the roughest rookeries of the East End, where it was understood that safety was a falsehood invented by those who had never experienced a moment of peril. But danger in her own territory—in this new fortress she had built where she ruled as king and queen both—was not something she had expected.

The Winter family had attracted notice and, subsequently, jealousy. That was the way of it in the East End. Do better, and everyone hates you. Do worse, everyone still hates you, and they'll stick a knife in your back just the same, but they won't hate you nearly as much.

Someone in her chamber? She had not expected that here. Not now. Her business had yet to even begin. *Hell*, there was every possibility she would fail, and that no fancy ladies would enter her establishment at all. But never mind that. If some bastard was keen on gutting her like a fish, she had a lesson for him. And it began with *don't try to cross Genevieve Winter*.

Slowly, she reached for the blade she kept beneath her pillow. Footsteps sounded on the floorboards. Not so damn subtle, this intruder. Her fingers found the cold metal, curving around the hilt.

Another creak sounded.

He was coming closer.

Nearer still.

In another step, he would be at her bedside. But she was prepared to do her worst. She gripped her weapon tighter, ready to pounce.

"Snoring, pet? I confess, I did not expect to hear it from you."

Pet?

That voice.

Sundenbury, curse his rotten, irritating, meddlesome, infuriating hide.

Her eyes flew open. "What the bloody fu—"

He pressed a finger over her lips. "Not now, empress. Oaths are ill becoming of a proper lady."

Empress, was it? Hardly better than *pet*. Had she thought to kill him with poison? Too lengthy a demise. Drowning would suffice. Or, even better, a blade between the ribs.

Glaring, she pulled her knife from beneath the pillow, holding it between herself and the marquess. "Get out of my room," she growled in warning.

But Blunderberry was unaffected by her threat. He flashed her his most charming smile, the one that showed off his bleeding dimples. His nose was slightly swollen this morning, but unfortunately, that imperfection did nothing to detract from his looks.

"No," he said pleasantly, as if she had issued a suggestion rather than a decree.

"You want your blood spilled today?" she demanded.

"Murderous wench. I ought to be granted additional pay for the damage to my person." His finger remained where it was, pressed over her lips, far too possessive and warm.

Like a brand, that damned touch.

With her free hand, she grasped his wrist, wresting him away. "You are not receiving pay, you arse. Because you have spent every ha'penny you possessed and then some. It is my goodwill that keeps you from the Suttons, and yet here you are, intruding on my privacy."

"Earning my keep, as it happens."

Was it wrong of her to notice how sinfully handsome the jackanapes was? Undoubtedly. Gen had one weakness, and it was the well-oiled charm of a gorgeous cove. But that did not mean she was unaware of her vulnerability.

"Difficult to earn your keep when you're a dead man."

"First, you broke my nose, and then you threatened my life. You are a Bedlamite, woman."

She glowered at his declaration. "Have to be one to agree to this stupid scheme. And your nose don't look broken, Blunderbury."

"Does not, pet." His grin deepened. "If you want to pretend you are a lady, you will have to take better care with your speech."

Ha! Just like a lord to fret over the way someone spoke. Everything she knew, she had taught herself. Growing up in the rookeries hadn't afforded her the chance to speak fancy. *Hell*, she was damned lucky she was still alive after the way she and Gavin had lived in their early years. After what her own mother had done. The old scar seemed to burn at the memory.

She pointed the tip of her blade at the scoundrel who had

invaded her territory. "And if you want to live to see another day, you'll get the hell out of my room."

He shrugged. "Not much left to lose. Don't think you're likely to slay the brother of your brothers' wives. The heir to the Duke of Linross, no less."

He was right, the devil, which rather nettled. As did the heat prickling her skin and settling between her thighs. Her body was a traitor. That much was certain. Fortunately, she had become skilled at ignoring it.

It was her turn to shrug. "Eh. I would not have to kill you. I could maim you."

But the action proved a mistake when it caused the bedclothes to drop to her waist. She was wearing an old linen shift, well-worn and soft. His gaze instantly dipped. Her nipples went hard. Her breasts felt heavy beneath the weight of that stare.

"So you *do* have a bosom beneath those gentleman's shirts and coats." His grin became a smirk as his eyes flicked back to hers. "I will own, I had wondered."

It required all the control she possessed to keep from clutching the counterpane to her chin like a frightened virgin. Instead, she remained still, giving him her most cutting look since she could not slice him like a cooked goose.

"Look again, and I'll blacken both your eyes," she warned.

"Afraid I will notice your nipples are hard, empress?" he goaded. "Too late for that, I am afraid. Your night rail is quite transparent."

Her fingers tightened on the hilt of her blade. "The air is cold, and the fire has gone out," she grumbled. "It has naught to do with you, Blunderbury."

"Liar."

The amusement fled his expression, and there was

nothing about the room or about Gen that was chilled in that moment. The air was aflame.

She had to do something.

So she pressed the blade to his chest. Not with enough force to draw blood, but enough to show him she had no intention of allowing him to remain here another moment. "Out of my chamber, lordling."

His tongue swept over his lower lip, and how she hated herself for following it. For wondering what that sensual aristocratic mouth would feel like against hers. Smooth, hot? Forceful or sweet? Gentle, tender, knowing? Awkward, unskilled, slippery?

Curse her mind for wondering. And curse it for also somehow knowing his kisses would never be the latter. Some gents kissed like fishes. Some like saints. The Marquess of Sundenbury, she could tell, kissed like a sinner.

She pressed harder with the blade.

Too hard.

The tip of her dagger pierced his shirt.

He howled and caught her wrist in a punishing grip. "Devil take it, woman. You drew my blood for the second time in as many days."

"I did not," she snapped. Typical cove, acting as if he had been dealt a mortal blow when she had not scarcely used enough pressure to...

Oh, hell.

A trickle of blood darkened the crisp whiteness of his shirt.

"You did," he informed her, grim.

"You ought to have been wearing a waistcoat. If you had been properly dressed, my blade never would have caused you so much as a scratch."

He moved swiftly, taking her by surprise, his fingers tightening on her wrist whilst the other hand plucked the dagger from her grasp. "That was hardly an apology, madam."

He tossed her blade over his shoulder and it clattered to the floor.

Her indignation soared, and she seized it. Because if she was angry, she could not dwell on the impossible longing circling within her. A longing, she was sure, that had far more to do with the length of time that had passed since she had been attracted to a man than it did with the irresponsible lord before her.

"Why should I apologize?" she demanded. "You are the one going about invading my office and my bedchamber. I agreed to keep you here and out of trouble. But I never said you could make free with my territory or my person."

His hands were on her upper arms now, and though his grip was firm, it was not punishing. Still, she could not escape him without doing him further damage, and she found herself reluctant to knee him in the ballocks. Gen was not certain why. Ordinarily, ruthlessness suited her. It was far preferable to weakness.

She had been weak once, long ago, when she had been too young to protect herself.

It had nearly been the end of her.

Never again.

"I am wounded." His stare was on her lips, his head lowering to hers, his voice deep and intimate, taking on a tone she imagined he reserved for his lovers. "Have you no mercy, empress?"

Empress.

She truly ought to rethink her lenience regarding her knee and his whore pipe.

"None for you," she told him. "Now go. There can be no lessons between us which require a bedchamber."

His golden-brown gaze darkened. The rapscallion's grin returned to his lips. "Oh, but there can be."

Her pulse fluttered. Something inside her which had been asleep woke. Her desire. The part of herself that was decidedly female.

Suddenly, his scent seemed to coil around her, rather in the fashion of a serpent. He smelled of citrus and bay. Fancy fragrances. Scents that spoke of his station. Although his papa the duke had cut off his purse strings, Lord Sundenbury was still an aristocrat. A man who had never known a moment of strife. A man who had never known the pangs of hunger in his belly, the icy fear of dread on the streets, the terror of wondering when someone would attack him in his sleep.

A reminder, that scent.

Her nostrils flared. "Get out, or I will spill more of your blood before the morning is over, Blunderbury."

His lips thinned. "Sundenbury. But you may call me Max. All my friends do. Foes, as well."

She was not a simpleton. The man was repeating her words, albeit in different fashion. "Max," she agreed, pleasantly enough. "Now do get the bloody hell out of my room."

He made a clucking sound with his tongue and shook his head. "I shall not shirk my duty in such egregious fashion. Our first lesson begins now, empress. That is why I am here, is it not?"

Did he mean here in her gaming hell or here in her chamber? In her bed?

Gen pursed her lips. "You are here by the grace of my goodwill."

"And mine. Do you truly believe most gentlemen would be eager to attempt to teach a bloodletting hellion such as yourself how to be a proper lady? That is the stuff of a governess, my dear. And not even a governess worth her weight in gold would take on such a lost cause."

"A lost cause, am I?" She raised a brow. "Mayhap I am. But I do not see much difference between us, Blunderbury. You are hiding in the East End to try to redeem yourself from years of playing the wastrel. I, however, am aiming to do something worthwhile."

"Hmm." His gaze dipped to her breasts once more.

"My face is not down there, lordling," she growled.

How dare he insult her as a lost cause and then ogle her bosom? If he weren't holding her in a manacle-like grip, she would have planted him another facer. Broken his beautiful beak for good.

Would he be as sinfully handsome with a crooked nose?

Yes, whispered a voice within. A voice she silenced.

"My favorite shade of pink," he said.

He was talking about her nipples, the rakehell. And instead of blasting him in the lordly splendor as she should, a wave of pleasure settled over her like a cloak. "You are impertinent, rude, and lingering where you do not belong."

"I was referring to the flush on your cheeks, empress. But do go on."

The flush he referred to went hotter still.

"Out, Blunderbury." She tugged, but his grip remained firm.

Uncompromising.

And his presence remained irksome. Tempting. Confusing.

"Not until we complete our first lesson." He had the audacity to wink at her then. "You do remember I am to teach you, do you not?"

Blast the rotter. Why had she agreed to this nonsensical plot?

"I begin to think there is nothing you can aid me with,

lordling. I'm bundling you on a carriage back to Mayfair just as soon as you get the hell out of my chamber."

"Oh, no, empress. You shan't be rid of me that easily." He grinned again.

By God.

The dimples had returned, and her heart refused to cease thudding.

"Yes I shall."

This time, she took action. Her knee, beneath the bedclothes. Quick. Not quick enough. He rose from the bed, releasing her, laughing.

"Our first lesson is in dressing like a lady," he informed her, before clapping his hands and calling over his shoulder. "Rose, we are ready for you now."

The door opened, and a beautiful woman crossed the threshold.

* * *

MAX MADE an absentminded pass over the slice in his shirt as he awaited Miss Genevieve Winter and Rose in the hall outside her chamber. Cozening the sought-after modiste to assist him in his plans had not been easy, but Rose was loyal. She had not forgotten the patronage of his mistresses, which had helped to establish her in London.

The latest wound Miss Winter had given him still stung. He could only hope she was not assaulting poor Rose over the notion she would be wearing skirts. It was a minor miracle he had persuaded the famed Madame Derosiers to visit a would-be gaming hell on the outskirts of the East End with a case of garments. If she left here with a broken nose on his account…

The door opened.

Max nearly swallowed his tongue at the vision standing

on the threshold. Ivory silk hugged her lush curves. The wicked decolletage of her gown put her bosom on display. And what a display it was—creamy skin, perfect handfuls, he had no doubt. He had known Gen Winter was beautiful. But dressed as she was, in one of Rose's confections, she could easily pass for a duchess.

"I'll not be going about dressed as a ladybird," she declared mulishly, quite dispelling the effect.

The moment Miss Winter opened her mouth, there was no mistaking her for a lady.

Max would be lying if he claimed that was not one of her most intriguing qualities. There was something about the brash female that was riveting. Alluring. Seeing her in bed this morning, her golden hair unbound, her bare arms, the hint of her pink nipples beneath that shift… It had done strange things to him.

And he was here to keep himself from trouble, not to fashion more of it. All the more reason to accomplish this Herculean task and carry on with the business of mending his relationship with his father. His new strategy was to make as much a lady of Miss Genevieve Winter as he could. With as much haste as possible.

"You look nothing like a ladybird, mademoiselle," Rose was reassuring her, thankfully taking no insult at Miss Winter's words. "You are *élégante. Très belle.*"

"I ain't wearing this sort of nonsense," growled his reluctant hostess. "Trousers are ever so much more comfortable than the contraption beneath this gown."

A surly thing, Miss Genevieve Winter. Stubborn, bloodthirsty, and irritable.

But if there was one thing Max excelled at—admittedly, it was *not* gambling—it was charming the fairer sex. Wooing, seducing, persuading: these were the skills he could claim as his own. Mayhap the only ones, aside from disappointing his family and becoming beholden to the wrong people.

Such as the Suttons and the Winters.

"The *contraption*, as you say, is a corset, Mademoiselle Winter, *nécessaire* for the proper shape. Lord Sundenbury, the corset is important for the silhouette, *n'est-ce pas*? Help me, *s'il vous plait*." Rose was frowning at him.

Dark-haired and chocolate-eyed, she was a true Gallic beauty. But even so, it was Miss Winter who stole all his attention. Rose had worked her hair into a clever chignon, which left burnished curls free to frame her face. There was a vulnerability in her countenance which had been absent before, and Max found himself drawn to this side of her. The side that was uncertain. Hesitant.

Their stares met and held, and he rubbed over the stinging flesh wound she had delivered to his chest.

"My lord?" Rose prodded.

The sharpness of irritation tinged her voice, reminding him she had been gracious enough to pay this call and he must not ignore her.

He flicked his gaze to the modiste, then back to Miss Winter. "It *is* important. Miss Winter, if you wish to attract a clientele from the upper echelons of high society, you cannot go traipsing about in trousers and men's boots."

"Why should they give a damn what I wear?" demanded Miss Winter, indignant.

Rose sighed. "Mademoiselle Winter, as a modiste, if I were to wear rags most *hideuse*, do you suppose anyone would have confidence in my abilities?"

Miss Winter frowned. "What's being dressed as a mollisher got to do with my ability to run a gaming establishment for ladies?"

A mollisher and a ladybird. *Christ*, if only the exasperating woman understood how expensive and sought-after Rose's designs were. But then, it was just as likely she would not give a damn.

"If you truly wish to attract ladies, you need to look like one, not just to speak like one, my dear," he intervened. "That is what Madame Derosiers is attempting to explain, and that is why I begged her to grace us with her presence and innate skill this morning."

"Hmm." Miss Winter gave him a guarded look. "I thought it was so you had an excuse to find your way into my room and ogle my bubbies."

Hell. His face went hot. But he refused to believe there was a flush spreading over his cheekbones, as if he were a virginal lad.

Rose made a strangled sound. "I am afraid I must go. You will keep what I have brought you, *oui*, Mademoiselle Winter? The ivory suits you. Pay me a call, and together we shall find a wardrobe fitting for you."

Miss Winter did not appear enthused. "Who is paying for this? Blunderbury is in Bushy Park. He'll not be affording it."

"In Bushy Park?" Rose's brow furrowed with confusion.

Max sighed, for he understood the flash Miss Winter had used. She was saying he was pockets to let. Which he was. "Madame Derosiers was kind enough to provide these to you, *gratis*."

Because he had pleaded. And because she owed him.

It was a favor he could not call upon again.

Miss Winter frowned. "*Gratis*? Is that some sort of fancy lord's word? And how much will *that* lighten my bloody purse?"

Of course she would have no knowledge of Latin. Max was frightfully ignorant of just what a woman who had been born and raised in the rookeries *would* know. Certainly, she would not have been raised to flourish at needlepoint or to pour a proper cup of tea. She would not have been coddled by a well-intentioned governess, and nor would she have been taught to speak other languages. Although her half brothers had married his sisters, Max's interactions with Mr. Dominic Winter and Mr. Devil Winter had been relatively limited.

Likely in part because of Max's admittedly disastrous problems. But he would not think of those just now.

"There is no cost, mademoiselle," Rose saved him by reassuring Miss Winter. "I am pleased to see one of my designs gracing a lady so fitting. These few gowns were commissioned by another, you see, until she became *enceinte*, necessitating new dresses and measurements."

"I ain't going to accept charity." Miss Genevieve Winter was, as usual, terribly blunt.

Bordering on rude, in fact.

"*I am not*," he corrected her. "Ain't is not what a proper lady would say, Miss Winter."

She sent him a scowl.

He wanted to kiss her.

By Hades, this latest scrape of Max's was not going to end well. There was a growing portent of impending doom filling the hall.

Rose cleared her throat. "Think of this not as charity, mademoiselle. I wish for you to try my creations. I hope you shall find them *acceptable*. Together, we can create more gowns to suit you."

The woman was a gem. Rose, that was. Not Miss Winter. Genevieve Winter was rather like a weapon. Sleek, beautiful, and dangerous. The wound on his chest throbbed then, as if in agreement, and so did his nose.

"I prefer trousers and boots, shirt and waistcoat." Miss Winter frowned some more. "Send the cost, if you please. Should you insist on leaving these items behind, you must be recompensed."

Max almost begged Rose to take the damned gown with her. Miss Winter was far too tempting in it. Like a confection he longed to devour. But he restrained himself. Instead, he offered to escort Rose to her carriage. The streets were not entirely safe on the edge of the East End, even at this morning hour. And he needed a few moments away from Miss Winter.

Moments during which he could hopefully tamp down the unwanted desire burning within him. The stubborn wench was still grumbling as Max escorted Rose below.

CHAPTER 3

Genevieve had found a quiet corner of her gaming hell to hide.

The kitchens, to be precise.

The table was broad and accommodating. She had drawn a reasonably comfortable chair to it. Her ledgers, ink, and pen in hand, she set to work, tallying her expenditures. Reading was not a strength of hers. However, arithmetic had always made sense to her mind. Numbers, she found, were not nearly as difficult to comprehend and decipher.

And she could not deny that the chance to be on her own was welcome. For the past three days, Lord Sundenbury had been chasing her about like a lonely puppy nipping at its master's heels. Only Blunderbury was significantly more irritating and deuced difficult to ignore.

But here, in the kitchens…why, it was heaven. No interloper in sight.

Indeed, no one was within at all, save her beloved dog Arthur, since the skilled French chef she had procured for her fledgling gaming hell was not within his sphere today.

Chef Armande was frightfully dear to procure, which meant she was having to share him with The Devil's Spawn, which was run by her half brother Dom.

Frowning down at her ledger, she wondered if she would need to bolster her wine stores. Or her gin? What did proper ladies drink? She would be damned if she was going to seek out bloody Sundenbury to ask. Having escaped him at all was merciful enough—

"I do believe it is time for our next lesson, Miss Winter."

"Blast," she bit out, jumping as she spun in her chair to find the lord in question stalking across the kitchens with his easy, long-limbed stride. The one that said he had been born a lord and everyone else could go to the devil.

Arthur, who was generally suspicious of everyone, rose from his place at her feet and moved to greet the marquess.

Sundenbury grinned, and the dreaded dimples made a return as he sank to his haunches to give Arthur a hearty scratch behind his ears.

"Good morning to you, sir," Sundenbury greeted.

Arthur's tongue lolled.

"Traitor," Gen grumbled. Then she added in a voice she was sure to carry, "He is a vicious beast, you know. Unpredictable. Never know when he will strike."

"And draw blood?" The marquess raised a brow, undeterred as he petted Arthur's neck. "Sounds rather similar to his owner."

Ever ready with a clever reply, the Marquess of Sundenbury. Ever charming, too, damn his hide. All the more reason for her to keep her distance. He had not even been haunting her establishment for a sennight, and already, he was causing her no end of difficulties. How could she possibly survive three more?

She frowned at him. "Keep your distance from the both of us, and your pretty lordly hide will be safe."

"Pretty?" He rose to his full height at last, his gaze smoldering. "Why, empress. I had no notion you have been ogling me."

Arthur barked, as if protesting the lack of attention he was suddenly receiving.

"You needn't fear for your virtue, Blunderbury," she said, skewering him with a narrow-eyed glare. "You aren't the sort of cove who interests me."

That was a lie. Part of the reason she had been keeping her distance was because the man was a terrible distraction. The last thing she needed was to be charmed by a wastrel aristocrat who could not keep away from the hazard table. Particularly this one. He was handsome as the devil and had managed to amass debts so deep, rival gaming hell owner Jasper Sutton had once sent men after him.

"No? What sort of man *would* interest Miss Genevieve Winter, I wonder?" His light query, issued as he closed the rest of the distance between them, made warmth unfurl in her belly.

His sort, apparently. Because Gen was a fool who had not learned her lesson well enough with the last rogue who had wooed her, stolen her heart, and smashed it to bits.

"None," she lied.

And then, the blighter proceeded to sit on the table, beside her ledgers. Still grinning. Dimples mocking her. "Nary a one?"

Only the most vexing one currently in the East End.

Gen settled her forgotten quill in its well and gritted her teeth. "Tell me, yournabs, are you addled in the head? Why is it you never sit on a bleeding chair?"

"Chairs are deuced boring." The grin deepened and those golden-brown eyes of his fairly sparked with mirth. And with something else, too.

Seduction.

She had a blade tucked into her boot, and she would use it if necessary. Arthur trotted back to her side and curled up at her feet with a sound of canine contentment. If only the little beggar could discern how much danger the fiend sitting upon her kitchen table presented.

One ear scratch, and he was smitten. But here was where she and her dog were decidedly different. Gen had no intention of allowing this cur to scratch her ears. Or anywhere else.

"Chairs are meant for arses," she informed Blunderbury. "If you are this confused about furniture, no wonder you are terrible at games of chance."

His grin faded, but he remained where he was, posed indolently on the table, elbow on one knee, long legs dangling. "Who says I am terrible?"

"Your debts."

He winced. "Lady Fortune abandoned me."

She raised a brow. "Your common sense abandoned your upper works, more like. Evidence: you are still seated upon a table."

"There is only one chair in sight, and you are in it. Would you have me sit on your lap, empress?" There was a lightness in his tone once more. A note of flirtation.

"You would crush me." She sniffed, which proved a grievous error as it brought his scent to her.

Why could he not smell terrible? And for that matter, why could he not be bracket-faced?

"Mayhap you would care to sit on my lap instead?" he suggested.

He was indeed flirting with her.

She scowled, as much at his wicked words as the reaction they prompted within her. A strange and decidedly unwanted burst of longing burned to life.

"This chair will do fine."

"Pity." He glanced down at her ledgers. "What is this?"

"Work." She crossed her arms over her chest, regretting the motion as it made her aware of her breasts in a way she ordinarily was not. "Something with which you are unfamiliar."

"*Au contraire*, Miss Winter. Look at me now. I am working off my debt and improving my reputation."

"Not too bloody well. All you've accomplished is annoying me and making one of your ladybirds give me some gowns and contraptions I have no intention of wearing."

"Madame Derosiers is not one of my ladybirds," he denied. "Jealous, empress?"

Of the dark-haired French beauty who owed him a favor? Disappointingly, yes.

"Never." She tipped up her chin. "You are keeping me from my work, Blunderbury. These ledgers won't tally themselves. I've more supplies to purchase for the opening of my gaming hell, and I need to be certain I have sufficient funds remaining. Not all of us spend more than we have, you see."

He tensed at her jab, and she knew a moment of regret at taunting him for his gambling failures.

"Not terribly sporting of you, Miss Winter. Behold: I am a new man. I have not attended the green baize since my last disastrous attempt at turning my luck around. Nor have I indulged in a sip of spirits."

Ah. That made sense. Gen had spent years at The Devil's Spawn, aiding her half brothers in running the gaming hell. Long enough to know the worst gamblers were the tap-hackled ones. The more they imbibed, the greater their losses. And that was why the poison was always freely flowing at every gaming establishment.

"Am I meant to give you applause?" she drawled, aware of how cutting she was being.

It was necessary to maintain a distance between them, however she could. Rudeness ordinarily proved a great success for her whenever she strove to keep a gentleman at bay. Wearing trousers and binding her breasts helped, too. Dressing as a lad had kept her safe when she and Gavin had been young, living on the streets of the rookery. It had done the same when she had required it to keep the patrons of The Devil's Spawn at a distance.

"I have a feeling there is nothing I could do—no feat I could possibly perform—that you would consider worthy of your applause." He slid from the table, landing effortlessly on his feet. "But I have sought you out for a different reason entirely."

Back to these lessons of his, were they?

"I am too busy for more of your nonsense today, my lord." She gestured toward the ledgers, which he was keeping her from. "Lessons can wait."

But he did not take his leave as she had hoped. Instead, he remained where he was. "I am afraid this particular lesson, more so than all the rest, cannot."

She stayed seated, refusing to budge. "Go bedevil some ladybirds."

"I do not know any ladybirds."

She snorted. "Your lying skills are as poor as your gambling skills, Blunderbury."

"You know, I am almost becoming fond of your sobriquet for me."

His flirtatious air had returned.

So had the sizzle in the air.

"I shall have to think of a worse one," she told him.

Her mind instantly went to work with possibilities.

Sundenbunny?

Sundenflurry?

Dunderbury?

"I doubt you could." His smile was once more in place. A lordly smile.

One that made her feel things.

Dreadful things.

"Lord Dunderhead," she decided, reminding herself to remain impervious.

He pursed his lips. "Unkind of you, empress. I thought we were friends."

"We are most definitely *not* friends." Outrage had her shooting from her chair. Arthur rose as well, rising on his three paws and glancing between his mistress and the interloper he had become so fond of.

"Nonsense. We *are* friends. Look at our ease with one another."

Ease. Was the man addlepated?

"We are not. I punched you in the nose and pricked you with my dagger. I don't like you."

"I think you do like me, Miss Winter." The marquess stepped nearer, crowding her with his tall frame.

With his scent.

With his handsome face.

She poked his chest with her forefinger. "You're touched in the head, you are."

Blast the man, but his warmth and the solid muscles lurking beneath his waistcoat and coat were both alarmingly alluring.

He caught her finger. "Careful now, empress. You may upset the last wound you dealt me, and it was just beginning to heal."

She would give him one to match. Blacken his eye.

Kiss him.

What the devil?

No. She would not kiss him. Not now. Not ever.

Gen tugged on her finger until he released it. "I don't like you at all, Dunderhead. Now if you please, leave me in peace before I have to call for Peter or ask Arthur to bite you."

"Not until we have our lesson. How am I to be successful if you continue to avoid me and your lessons both?"

Precisely.

"I am a busy woman," she said simply.

"You asked for my aid," he countered.

Yes, she had. But that had been before she knew what he looked like. And sounded like. And smelled like.

"Your persistence is bloody annoying," she told him.

"So I have been told before." The grin returned. "Sometimes, it has gotten me into trouble. Other times, it has proven a boon."

"You are not going to leave me in peace, are you?"

Dimples appeared. "Not a chance."

"Fine." She scowled at him, trying to ignore the flutter in her belly. "Let us have the lesson, then, so you can be gone."

"Capital idea. Come with me, empress."

* * *

MAX FACED Miss Winter in the blue gaming room, which was the largest of all the hell's chambers. "Here we are."

"Where have you taken my tables and chairs?" she demanded curtly.

Of course that was her first reaction. He ought to have expected it. The woman was devoted to her business. She worked hard, from morning until night, and she fretted after those in her employ and the most minute details of the gaming hell.

"Never fear, empress," he reassured her, "they have been

carefully removed to the golden room. They will be returned to their exact positioning when our lesson is at an end."

Her gaze was withering, her expression skeptical. "You never did say what manner of lesson this is to be. If you send in another Frenchwoman with cases of gowns, I'll blacken your eye."

He had no doubt she would.

Max hid his smile, for as much as he enjoyed nettling his prickly hostess, he wanted her to cooperate with him. Push her too far, and she might well flee. Today's lesson was an important one. Also, it was an excuse to get her in his arms. He would not lie.

"No Frenchwoman," he assured her. "I vow."

"What is it then? I fail to see what manner of lesson would require the removal of my damned furniture."

"You really ought to consider reducing your epithets, my dear," he counseled, trying to envision the reaction the ladies of his acquaintance would have to a knife-wielding, trousers-wearing woman with the lexicon of a pirate.

"Hmm."

He ignored her glare. "Today's lesson is dancing."

"Dancing?" she spat the word as if it, too, were another of her favored curses.

"Correct."

"No." She crossed her arms over her chest as she had done earlier in the kitchens, glaring. "I'll have no need to do something so foolish here. I was right, you are a Bedlamite."

He had anticipated this response. He was ready for her.

"Dancing is about movement, grace, elegance. It will help you to move with poise. To be a lady."

"Never said I wanted to be a lady."

He suppressed a sigh. "Of course not. You merely want to play a part so you can fool all the unsuspecting females you intend to lure here so you may relieve them of their pin money."

"Yes." She beamed at him, looking pleased.

It felt as if a massive hand were squeezing his heart. That lovely face sans scowl was undeniably breathtaking. She was maddening. Stubborn. Unique. He wanted her with a ferocity that surprised him. Left him bemused.

He forced his mind back to the subject at hand, which had nothing to do with seducing Miss Genevieve Winter and everything to do with his true reason for being here.

"Learning to dance—and to dance well—is imperative," he informed her.

He thought she might offer further argument. *Good Christ*, the woman was more combative than a regiment of soldiers in battle, fighting to the death. However, she offered no quarrel.

Instead, she cocked her head, considering him with those bright-blue eyes. "And how shall we dance without music, my Lord Dunderhead? Never tell me there is a dancing master somewhere in London who also owes you a favor."

He laughed. "Not quite. But we shall have music nonetheless. What say you, Miss Winter? May I have the honor of this dance?"

He swept into an elaborate bow just as he would on any society ballroom floor.

She did not laugh at him, which was an excellent sign.

When he rose, he found her looking adorably befuddled. Standing there in her trousers, shirtsleeves, and waistcoat, her boots shined, her hair caught in a thong at her nape, she was majestic.

"What do you want me to do, you daft rogue?" she asked.

And nor had she issued an oath. Also promising.

He held out his hand to her. "Come nearer, if you please. We are going to dance the waltz."

"The waltz?" Her brow furrowed. "What is that?"

"A scandalous dance. You will like it, I promise." He winked at her, hoping she would play along.

Not just because he did not have more lessons in mind, but because he wanted her to relax. To dismantle her guard. To allow him to hold her close and guide her about the room.

"Forgive me, sir, but my brothers have told me that is the last phrase I should ever believe when issued from a man." Her gaze was shrewd.

Not wrong, her brothers.

He feigned a cough to cover his startled chuckle. "I am here with your brothers' blessing."

"Because their wives are convinced you are not entirely the devil."

His sisters loved him, and he loved them. *Good God*, Addy had embroiled herself with Dominic Winter to save him, and though he would have stopped her, he still appreciated her efforts on his behalf.

"And what do you suppose, Miss Winter? Do you think I am entirely the devil?"

"I am not afraid of you, Marquess."

Dare he be hopeful at her lack of insulting sobriquet?

"If you are not afraid of me, then prove it," he urged, sensing the opportunity. Miss Genevieve Winter was like a gamble herself. Only this time, he was wagering his pride instead of his funds. "Dance with me."

Her lips tightened with displeasure. She was reluctant about this, there was no doubt. But she sighed, the sound steeped in resignation.

"Very well. Just this once, and no more." Miss Winter took a step nearer.

"Closer," he urged, trying to stay the furious rush of desire within.

She moved again. He slid his arm around her waist and

drew her toward him, until they were almost flush against each other. And then he guided her hand around him, before catching the other and lacing their fingers together and raising them above their heads.

"I will step on your feet," she warned.

He bit back a smile. "Do your worst, empress. You shan't hurt me, I promise."

Max could have kissed her then, but he did not. He began to hum. A fairly convincing waltz, he felt. He had an excellent singing voice and he knew it. One of few victories he could claim, as it happened.

"*You* are the music?"

A mere lowering of his head, and his lips would seal with hers. But she was skittish. She required further wooing, and he knew it. There was something about Genevieve Winter which was not just different.

Original.

The word came to him, and he seized it, for the descriptor was apt. He knew instinctively he would never meet another woman like her.

He stopped humming. "Yes, I am the music. Do you mind? I have been told my voice is passable on more than one occasion."

"Oh." Her gaze had fallen to his mouth. She blinked, a tinge of pink on her cheekbones as she swallowed and seemed to collect herself. "Your voice is…pleasant enough, I suppose."

Ha! High praise indeed coming from Miss Genevieve Winter. He would take it.

And he had decided he would take *her*.

But not yet. He had time for that. Three more weeks. And longer, a man could hope. He did not think three weeks with this woman would be nearly sufficient.

"Then I shall burden your ears with my humming, and

you shall follow my lead," he told her.

Without waiting for her to answer, he took action, humming and guiding them in a turn. He had never taught anyone to dance before, and Christ knew he was far from a dance master, but he reasoned the movements and the rhythm would be easiest to learn first. Then the steps.

However, he quickly discovered he was wrong.

Their feet somehow became intertwined, and she tripped him. Max narrowly avoided taking a tumble to the floor and dragging her down too.

"Perhaps some footwork first," he decided.

"I attended a ball once, you know," she said, chin going up in pugnacious fashion.

He could not contain his surprise. "You did?"

"Aye." She gave a jerky nod. "Wore a gown, too. Just two months ago, it was. The Christmastide celebration at Abingdon Hall."

Ah, yes. That would make sense. The Winter family celebrations.

"Did you dance?" he asked.

"No." She looked sheepish as she made the admission. "I am a hopeless cause, Blunderbury. Even you must admit it."

"I do not acknowledge defeat."

"Little wonder you lost all your money at the Sutton hell," she said.

And she was not wrong.

How could he explain the thrill wagering his blunt had given him? All his life, he had been hounded by his father. Molded and shaped and told what to do. Reprimanded for the slightest infraction. *You are the future duke*, was the reminder, the incessant rebuke. *You are the heir*.

But he had never been good enough for his father. Too stupid, too loud, too lazy. Too much the opposite of the mold his father would have made him in. Gaming, taking chances, drinking, whoring—those had become his solaces.

Until he had lost himself along the way, and until he had almost lost his sisters as well.

"I deserve that," he acknowledged. "And you are right in noting there were many occasions in my past where I should have admitted defeat and surrendered. However, this is not one of them."

"There are likely chickens you could teach to dance with greater ease than myself."

"Yes, but would the chickens insult me, knock me in the nose, and threaten me with knives?" he teased.

She pursed her lips, the action not doing one thing to aid his restraint. "Are you saying you find me entertaining, Dunderhead?"

Massively.

And delicious. But he was keeping that to himself for now.

"I am saying that you are interesting. That is all." He renewed his determination to teach her to dance. "But that is quite enough chatter for now, Miss Winter. We have a waltz to dance."

"Hmm," was all she said.

Not a curse. Nor an insult.

"Watch my feet," he instructed. "We shall go slowly this time."

Then, he began guiding them. She stepped on his toes thrice. Having her in such proximity was pure torture. She smelled of flowers. A garden in bloom. Her scent was completely at odds with the rest of her. A mystery wrapped in a conundrum.

"Forgive me," she said when she trampled his toes a fourth time. "Surely you must see I am a hopeless cause."

"Do you think *I* am one, Miss Winter?" he asked her, quite seriously, forcing her to hold his stare.

She did not look away. Brilliant blue dazzled him.

"No," she admitted at last. "I do not believe anyone is, including you, Marquess."

He could work with that. Yes, indeed.

"Then let us keep trying." He tightened his grip on her waist. She was not wearing gloves—of course she wasn't—and the sensation of her bare skin upon his was driving him to the edge of madness. "Follow the beats. One, two, three..."

They worked in pained silence for a few minutes. A few more mishaps occurred. But at last, they began to move with greater fluidity. Miss Winter seemed to be grasping the motions.

"Where is the music?" she asked after a time.

Once more, he suppressed his smile. Obligingly, he began to hum, and they moved about the room, whirling as one. Several missteps later, their dance became almost elegant. Their bodies were in unison, and there was an inherent rightness about holding this woman in his arms, about dancing with her. She was a quick study, Miss Genevieve Winter. He could not say he was surprised.

However, when they moved into the faster portion of the dance, arms closer around each other, spinning in circles as they navigated the room, their feet became tangled once more. This time, there was no correcting his balance. They tumbled together, Max scarcely managing to turn them so he bore the brunt of the fall. He landed on his back, with Miss Winter atop him. He loved the weight of her, the collision of her feminine curves with his masculine planes.

Her palms flattened on his chest. Her face hovered over his, eyes wide.

"Seems we took a spill," she said, sounding breathless.

Very interesting indeed.

Miss Genevieve Winter was surly. She was claws and bared teeth and growls. She was not breathless. Except she was now, and he loved that, too.

"You are hell-bent upon injuring me, are you not?" he teased.

A gentleman would have let her go. But Max's hold on her tightened, making certain she would stay where she was. Since when had he been a gentleman?

"I am innocent this time, I swear it." She was smiling back at him, stealing his own breath.

Making his heart thud in his chest.

Forcing a bolt of desire straight to his hardening cock.

He gritted his teeth to stave off a fresh wave of longing and attempted to resituate her so that she would not feel the effect she was having upon him. "You may trip me any time you like, Miss Winter. Just as long as you promise to fall into me."

Her lips parted. She wriggled against him, and the friction over his burgeoning erection had him biting his inner cheek to keep from groaning. It also made his state apparent to her. He knew it the moment her eyes widened and she ceased all movement.

More heat engulfed him.

He could not recall ever experiencing an attraction this strong, this deep. It should be absurd. He should not want her so much. And yet, he could no more extinguish the feelings roaring through him than he could expunge the sun from the sky. It was that bold, that bright, that necessary.

But just when he thought he saw her softening, her head dipping nearer, her mouth closer to his, she pushed away from him.

"Thank you for the lesson, Marquess."

"Miss Winter—"

She scrambled away from him as if he were fashioned of flame. "My ledgers are waiting."

Damn it.

He sat up, rueful. "Miss Winter, if you please…"

His words trailed off. She was already flitting over the threshold as if their entire encounter had never been. The persistent ache within him told a different story.

He wanted Genevieve Winter.

But could he have her? That was the question.

CHAPTER 4

Gen woke to scratching on her door.
And whining. Then a bark.
Arthur.

She sat up in bed, wondering why he was not settled down in his bed by the kitchens, where he preferred to sleep because he was often gifted scraps. That was when she noticed a scent on the air...

Smoke.

More barking, more scratching.

Smoke meant there was a fire.

She vaulted from her bed and raced across her room, terror lodged in her chest. She had not even reached the door when it burst open. Her chamber filled with the glow of a candle as Arthur ran to her, nimble on his three legs.

"Miss Winter!"

A familiar, masculine figure filled the doorway.

The marquess.

"Miss Winter, you must come with me," he said, extending a hand. "We haven't much time."

"What is happening?" she demanded. "Where are my men?"

"There is a fire. Peter is manning the fire buckets. I came to see you safely outside."

There was a fire in her gaming hell—which had yet to open—and he imagined she was going to follow him to the street whilst everyone else fought to save it?

"No."

"Damn it, woman, there are times to be stubborn. This is not one of them."

Desperation edged his voice as he stormed forward, as if he intended to bodily haul her from the room and edifice altogether.

"I will fight the fire with my men," she told him, hastening toward her wardrobe, so she could change out of her shift and don some trousers and a shirt. It wouldn't do to attempt to fight a blaze whilst wearing a gown. One wrong move, and the bleeding thing would catch flame.

"I cannot allow that. It is not safe." Sundenbury was behind her.

She did not give a shite if he was still in the room. Ignoring him, she grasped her shift in two fistfuls of linen and ripped it over her head before whipping it to the floor. Cool night air kissed her bare arse but she was too beset by fear to care.

"Genevieve."

"Stay where you are, Dunderhead. I am naked as a babe."

"I am aware." His tone sounded strangled.

Shouts rose below and her heart quickened, mouth going dry. Fire was destructive—a nightmare for anyone. The Devil's Spawn had suffered damage in the past by flame, but they had emerged fortunate. She had yet to even attract a single lady to her establishment. If it burned to ashes before she had a chance, everything would be over.

She would be ruined.

And if any of her men were injured or worse in this blaze...

She refused to think it.

Gen pulled her shirt over her head, then stuffed her legs into trousers. She fastened the buttons on the fall before spinning back to face the marquess. Arthur was on the floor between them, whining and barking. He was ever a protective beast. But in this instance, it almost seemed as if he was protecting the both of them.

"Where are the flames?" she asked. "Has the fire brigade been called?"

"The kitchens, and yes." He was frowning at her.

The devil was handsome even in the shadows, his hair disheveled quite as if he had run his fingers through it in distress. "Right. Take Arthur and wait on the street. Wouldn't do for me to be responsible for the death of a princely lord."

In truth, she wanted him—and her beloved dog—safe. A man like Lord Sundenbury would only be an encumbrance in a situation like this. She needed him out of the way so she could concentrate on the task at hand. Namely, saving her business and everyone she employed both.

Her boots were on her feet and she was rushing across the room.

The marquess followed her, Arthur on their heels. Down the hall, then the stairs. Smoke was getting thicker as they progressed. The shouts of distress louder. She was not going to lose her hell. Nor one single soul.

She vowed it.

"Damn you, Genevieve." The marquess stalked after her, following as she made her way toward the kitchens.

Gen's mind raced. How could there have been a fire? The chef had been absent today. Every meal which had been served had been cold. No fire in the grate when she had been within, settling her ledgers. Nor should there have been one.

Nothing about this made sense.

The taste of suspicion mimicked the bitterness of fear in her mouth. A wall of smoke greeted them as they reached the hall leading to the kitchens. She turned to the marquess, placing a staying hand on his arm. "I meant what I said, Marquess. Take Arthur and go to where it is safer. I'll not have my dog getting lost in the smoke because you are too stupid to listen to reason."

"Tell me which one of us is racing toward the flames and I will tell you which of us is not listening to reason." He was scowling at her now, waving distractedly at the smoke billowing around them. "Please, Genevieve. Come with me. The men are doing all they can, and if the fire is too far gone, your presence will not be sufficient to aid them. All you will do is get yourself hurt or worse in the process."

"And who would care if I do?" she snapped. "Go, lordling. You are neither wanted nor needed here. You will only be in the way. You *are* in the way."

Arthur barked. The marquess took her arm.

"Genevieve, please. This is madness."

"I protect what is mine," she told him.

And she did. From the time she and her brother Gavin had been old enough to remember, they had been taking care of each other. No one else had given a damn about them, especially not their mother. When they found the rest of the Winters, their family had expanded. Now, she had those she employed here as yet another part of her family.

Bonds were important to Gen.

So was saving this damned hell and everyone within it.

She stalked past Sundenbury, coughing and choking on the thick smoke as she made her way into the kitchens.

Within, she found—blessedly—only smoldering rubble. No flames. Peter, who had been a trusted friend something in the vein of a brother to her for these many years now, was at the helm. Fire buckets were traveling down a line, the men dousing the ruins of the kitchen table and nearest wall.

Lamps were lit far enough from the origin of flame to cast light upon their labor but not near enough that they would become imperiled should the flames have grown. It was, surprisingly, a scene of calm.

Like the quiet of the streets after a rainstorm.

It never lasted long.

"Peter!" She reached his side, waving at the thickened air before her in an attempt to dispel it. "What has happened?"

"Fire," he clipped. "Started 'ere in the kitchens. 'isnabs was awake and 'eard glass smashing. Thought to wake us all. Good thing is, we 'ad a line of fire buckets. Fire brigade 'asn't come yet, and already 'ave it out, we do."

And before she had even raised a hand to help them in their efforts. Shame washed over her, along with relief. The two intertwined.

Until the entirety of what Peter had just relayed to her settled into the cracks and crevices of her agitated mind. *Hisnabs* had been the one to note something was amiss.

She turned to Sundenbury, who was once more a grim specter at her side, Arthur adoringly lingering at their feet. "You are the one who discovered the fire?"

He nodded, clenching his jaw. "Yes. But I am not the one who fought it."

"I sent 'im to see that you were safe, miss, soon as I seen what we were up against." Peter shook his head. "If 'e wouldn't 'ave told us about the fire, every one of us would 'ave been burnt right up."

Her eyes were burning. Remnants of the fire, she told

herself. It was everywhere, hanging thick, coiling around them. The hot, charred carcass of her kitchens seemed to mock her. And yet, when her gaze locked with the Marquess of Sundenbury, a man she knew to be a wastrel who could not keep himself from trouble, something inside her shifted. A new awareness burst to life, one not just founded in the physicality of his beauty. That, she could not deny. But instead based upon something of far greater import to Gen.

Respect.

Tonight, the marquess had saved not just her hell from destruction, but he had also saved the lives of so many others, including Gen and Arthur.

She was humbled. Grateful. She inhaled deeply in an attempt to calm herself, but the hot smoke curled into her lungs, making her choke and sputter and cough. When at last she could properly breathe again, she wiped the tears from the corners of her eyes.

"Thank you," she managed. "Both of you. Thank you to each one of you. I will never forget this night. Not as long as I live."

Arthur barked, as if to concur.

"Another round of buckets!" called one of the men. "We need to be certain this sodding fire is done!"

"Aye," Peter agreed. "More buckets."

Gen stood in line and took a fire bucket from one of the stable boys. "I'll help."

The marquess, much to her surprise, settled into the line as well. Behind her.

"As will I," he said.

The line went back to work. Each of them, together.

* * *

As dawn rose over the East End, Max escorted Arthur and Miss Winter back to her rooms. It had taken hours, along with the late arrival of the fire brigade, and much difficult labor, to make certain the fire was altogether doused. The smoldering coals had been prodigious in their attempts to reignite, but their tedious efforts had prevailed.

"I am sorry about what happened this evening," he told her, feeling her anguish at the destruction which had been wrought quite keenly.

As if it were his own, in fact. The agony on her face for a brief moment as she had surveyed the ultimate damage to her kitchens had felt like a blade piercing his heart. But in typical Miss Genevieve Winter fashion, she did not shed a tear. Nor did she betray a hint of her inner devastation after schooling her features into their customary, impervious mask.

"You needn't be sorry," she said quietly as they stopped at the threshold of her private apartments. "If you hadn't been aware, if you hadn't taken note of the crashing and the flames…"

He suppressed a shudder as his mind traveled to the same, dark place.

Every one of them could have lost their lives in such a blaze, had it taken root and grown beyond the kitchens. And even more frightening—to think someone could have started the fire intentionally, with just such an evil intention. But he would not express his concerns to her now. The sun was rising, and she was soot-stained and fatigued.

She had almost lost her gaming hell this evening. And her life as well.

"I am relieved if I played any part in keeping your hell from burning down," he told her.

"The noise you heard," she began.

"Later, empress," he interrupted gently, a sudden fierce

burst of protectiveness toward her overcoming him. "You need some rest."

She shook her head, the obstinacy he had come to know so well in their short acquaintance presenting itself in the sudden harshness of her expression, the rigidity of her jaw. "Not yet. I want to know about the breaking glass. Did you see anything? Anyone?"

He shook his head. "No. I was not near enough. By the time I reached the kitchen, the flames had already begun."

"Someone started the fire intentionally," she said then, echoing his thoughts. "There was no fire in the kitchens all day. No one should have been within. Everyone I employ is loyal. I know each one of them well. They are trustworthy to a man."

How well did she know them? He could not help but to wonder, with a twinge of jealousy he could not control. Her relationship with Peter seemed... *Hell.* Peter worshipped the ground upon which Genevieve Winter trod. That much was apparent. As did every last man beneath this roof.

Max included. The woman astounded him.

Tonight, she had been a warrior, running headlong into danger, standing in line with her men, staying awake till dawn, when at last they had all dispersed to varying corners of the hell, their faces blackened, their bones weary if the way Max felt was any indication. He felt as if he could sleep for a solid sennight.

But she was still watching him, waiting, it seemed, for a response.

"Do you have enemies, Miss Winter?" he asked.

She pursed her lips, thinking. "Suttons. There was Paul Wilmore, but he's been dead for a year now. Mayhap more. Haven't heard a bit from his mongrels since then."

Max knew the Suttons. He had gambled in their hell. Had lost a staggering sum there. He had also frequented

Wilmore's establishment at one point, until it had ceased its operations. At which point he had ventured back to the Suttons' Sinner's Palace, although he had been strongly discouraged from gaming there, and where he had lost everything he had left, including his own self-respect.

He paused, pondering over that information. "The Suttons are a rival of the Winters, are they not?"

"Aye." She nodded, weariness lining her countenance once more before she straightened her shoulders and cast it away. "We have been rivals. Jasper Sutton is a bloody bastard and a thieving scoundrel capable of doing anything, if you ask me. My brothers have been deceived by his claims of truce, but I ain't about to believe it."

"Would the Suttons have attempted to destroy your hell?"

She sighed. "Don't know. Damn these bastards. Until today, the worst problem I expected to face was attempting to lure fancy ladies here to empty their reticules. But now…"

Now, it seemed she had an enemy who was hell-bent upon razing her gaming hell before it had even had the chance to open.

"Miss Winter," he began, seeking to comfort her and then faltering.

"Cease the *Miss Winter*, damn you." She bit out a laugh that sounded as if it were one-half sob. "Look at me. Look at you. I am covered in dirt, as are you."

"Gen," he relented. "I am sorry."

"For what?"

Her demand cracked like a whip through the stillness between them, which had fallen so strangely and unexpectedly after the bustle and intensity of the last few hours. So many people, faces, voices, clamoring and working together in a united cause.

"I am sorry some bastard attempted to destroy this place.

Sorry I did not interrupt the miscreant before he could set fire to the kitchens. Sorry for the fright you had tonight."

"I ain't afraid of anything, Marquess."

She was clinging to her defenses once more. Attempting to rebuild the walls which had been dismantled during the course of the night. He was having none of that. He had made it this far. She was not going to slam the door upon him now.

"Your fearlessness is commendable, my dear, but that alone will not be sufficient to vanquish whatever foe is determined to destroy you," he warned her. "You will have to make a plan. We need to find out who was behind tonight's attack on your establishment."

"We?" Her chin went up in defiance. "I don't reckon I asked you for help, Marquess."

She was a prideful woman, and he admired that in her as well. She was fierce in her determination to maintain her independence, to be the ruler of her own domain. Max was not intimidated by her zealous leadership, however. If anything, it drew him to her more. He could truly, honestly say he had never met a woman in his life who could compare to Genevieve Winter when it came to determination, bravery, and daring. Except, mayhap, for his sisters Addie and Evie. The twins had managed to find their own ways, it was true.

"You do not need to ask for my help," he countered. "I wish to give it, freely."

"And how much aid can a duke's wastrel son be to me?" She frowned at him, looking vexed.

Her question stung.

He stepped nearer to her. "How quickly your gratitude fades, empress."

"My gratitude has not faded," she said. "Forgive me. It's

been a long day and I am...bloody hell, I don't know what I am anymore. Thank Christ no one was hurt or worse."

Indeed.

Arthur whined at their feet. The hound had not left his mistress's side since the fire. He was a fiercely protective dog.

"Loyal little lad," he said, hunkering down to give Arthur a thorough scratch behind the ears. "He was locked away, barking and scratching like mad when I rushed to find you, and then he raced off to your apartments when I released him."

She frowned down at him. "Arthur was locked away?"

Max rose to his full height once more. "Yes."

She muttered something beneath her breath.

He did not suppose it was something kind, so he didn't deign to request clarification. He expected to have far more opposition from her before he was finished here.

Best to get on with it.

He took a deep breath. "Miss Winter, I do not think you should sleep alone."

Her mouth dropped open. For an indeterminate span of time, she stared at him, unspeaking.

And then she began to laugh. Uproariously.

She laughed until tears were streaming down her cheeks, taking the remnants of soot with them, and then she dashed at her cheeks. "And who is it you reckon ought to sleep with me, Marquess? You?"

"Yes, as it happens." Because he was the only bloody man beneath this roof he trusted not to attempt to bed her.

For now.

As in gambling, wooing a woman was all about timing. Too bloody bad he was terrible at the green baize. When it came to seducing the fairer sex, he was far more adept.

"No."

He had known she would protest, of course. Max had

been turning this scenario over in his mind as their duty on the fire line had dwindled and finally come to an end. He was prepared with a sound argument.

"Someone tried to burn down your establishment tonight," he pressed. "You are weary and vulnerable. The kitchen is scarcely secured, in ruins as it is. You should not be alone."

"Alone is the only way I'll sleep, Marquess. Go and tup your ladybird if you need to get the poison out."

By God.

"Get the poison out?"

"Making the beast with two backs," she elaborated. "Do the feather-bed jig. Whatever you like to call it. I ain't letting you into my bed."

Had there ever existed a woman quite like her? Max sincerely doubted so.

His father would be appalled to hear a female with such a vulgar tongue. Max couldn't lie; her disregard for all things polite was refreshing. And enough to keep his cock half-hard whenever he was in her presence.

That would wait.

Timing, he reminded himself.

"No making of a beast or jigs shall be conducted, empress," he told her, keeping the levity from his expression by exerting the utmost will.

If he laughed at her, she was likely to plant him a facer. And he was utterly serious about her welfare. He had no intention of leaving her alone. She could be as stubborn as she liked. He was resting in her chamber for the next few hours, and so was Arthur.

"Ha! That's what all the coves say. Then they're trying to ram their tongues down your throat and put your hand on their pego."

Fury lanced him. "Who has dared to do that to you?"

He would find every one of them and blacken their eyes.

She shook her head. "No one for some time. I learned to protect myself. That's why I don't need you, Marquess. Go to your room. Get some sleep."

That was not happening.

"Arthur and I will sleep on the floor." He glanced down at her three-legged canine, who was as animated and active as any dog he had ever met with all four legs. "Eh, lad?"

Arthur barked obediently. *That's a good lad.*

Max raised a brow and gave her a meaningful look. "You see? Arthur agrees with me."

"He's a beast."

As am I when it comes to you, my dear Miss Winter.

But he didn't say that. Instead, Max smiled his most charming smile, the one that showed his dimples to perfection. He did not think even Miss Genevieve Winter was impervious.

"A beast who understood you were under siege this evening, Miss Winter. He led me to you. He trusts me. You should as well."

Well, mayhap not as mindlessly as her hound, but Max kept that bit to himself. Instead, he held his breath, awaiting her response.

Her eyes narrowed in that suspicious glare of hers he had come to recognize. "Arthur is too trusting."

"Arthur saved you," he countered.

"One could argue you did. You already know where my rooms are. You didn't need him to guide you."

She was not wrong. And her words were a beacon of light when he least expected it. Interesting. Promising, as well? He dared to entertain the hope.

"I was acting on behalf of your hound," he said modestly. "But now, I am acting on behalf of myself and everyone else beneath this roof. We want to make certain you are safe.

Someone is trying to destroy your lady's gaming hell before it has even opened its doors. That someone has proven himself deuced dangerous this evening. I cannot, as a gentleman, leave you here in good conscience. So you see? You must agree, else I shall be heartbroken. Arthur as well. Is that not right, old chap?"

He issued the last question to her dog, who offered a bark of acquiescence.

"I have a blade," Miss Winter said. "More than one. I also have a brace of pistols. I can maim or kill a cove in the blink of an eye."

He had no doubt she could. Or that she did. Indeed, had she proclaimed she possessed a full arsenal of cannon and infantrymen and cavalry as well, he would not have been surprised in the least. It seemed the sort of thing Miss Genevieve Winter would have and do.

But he met her gaze, unwavering. "To hell with your blade and pistols. Let me be your guard. If anyone should bluster his way in here, he will deal with me first and give you time to protect yourself."

She cocked her head, considering him. "Not a bad point, Marquess. The floor, you say?"

He bit back an exuberant surge of glee at her capitulation. This woman did not lower her defenses with ease, and he knew it. And appreciated it, and her, too. "The floor. With Arthur. The both of us will protect you."

"Arthur does not prefer to sleep here," she countered.

"He does tonight." He lowered his gaze to the dog in question. "Do you not, lad?"

Arthur stared up at him.

"Lad?"

Arthur barked.

Max grinned at Miss Winter. "You see? Even the hound agrees."

She sniffed. "Very well. If you must. But I meant what I said. No blanket hornpipe, Dunderhead."

Blanket hornpipe?

Christ.

Max nodded, swallowing down his laughter and objections both. "Fair enough."

CHAPTER 5

Gen was not the kind who resorted to waterworks.

But standing in the ruins of her gaming hell's kitchens by the light of day was prompting the troublesome prickle of unwanted emotion. Her eyes were watering. She blinked furiously, trying to send the damned tears back to the devil where they belonged.

But her vision had gone hazy, and the cursed things showed no sign of retreating.

"Do you know what I do whenever I lose?"

She turned at the familiar voice to find the masculine shape of Sundenbury sauntering toward her. She thought she had left him sleeping on the floor of her room with Arthur. Yet here he was, the soot scrubbed from his face to reveal achingly sharp cheekbones and that rigid jaw her fingers itched to caress.

Clearly, her weakness was getting the better of her. Lusting after the marquess as she stood in the charred remnants of all her aspirations.

She gritted her teeth, recalling his query. "I haven't lost. This is an impediment to my goals. Nothing more."

In truth, she was blustering. She had sunk everything she had into the success of this gaming hell. The cost of the repairs to her kitchens alone could be enough to render her gaming hell an impossibility without the aid of her brothers. And she had so desperately wanted to make this come to fruition on her own, using nothing but the funds she had amassed over the years through her earnings at The Devil's Spawn.

"I was not suggesting this is a defeat." He stopped before her, unfairly handsome. "I was comparing my failures and the way they left me feeling to the way you must be feeling now as you stand here surrounded by the carnage of your kitchens."

Carnage. Aye, that was the word for it.

She was unamused. "I can guess what you do when you lose, Marquess. You bet again, and you lose again."

He inclined his head. "That was the old Sundenbury. The new Sundenbury no longer gambles."

"And birds do not have wings," she grumbled, not believing him for a moment.

She knew his sort well. She had grown to womanhood surrounded by gentlemen just like him—fancy lords who had nothing better to do with their time than throw away their blunt on gaming, liquor, and whores.

He shrugged. "Believe what you wish. However, I will tell you my secret. Whenever anything happens to me that I do not like—a loss at the tables, for instance—I find something which makes me laugh."

She glared at him. "Laugh?"

"Laughter is an excellent means of distracting one's self."

"So is singing, but I ain't about to throw off a rum chaunt just now. Have a bloody look around you."

His lips twitched.

She scowled. "Are you laughing at me, Dunderhead?"

He grinned. Dimples in full, splendid force. "It depends upon whether or not my admission will result in a knife wound or an empress-sized fist to the nose."

He truly was the most ridiculous man. She wanted to kiss him. And that confounded Gen. So she reacted. Scooped up a handful of whatever was nearest—ashes, as it happened—and tossed it at his chest. His crisp, white shirt was covered in dirt.

That pleased her. "That is what it shall result in, Marquess. Leave me to my misery or I will dump the next bit over your head."

His eyebrows raised. "Do you dare threaten me?"

Oh, she dared. The man was…meddlesome. Irritating. She liked him far more than she should and a hell of a lot more than she had anticipated she would. Which meant he was trouble.

She grabbed another fistful of ashes and tossed it toward him. "You are banished from the kitchens. Get out."

But instead of heeding her, Sundenbury took up a handful of soot himself and tossed it at Gen. It landed on her waistcoat. Her *favorite* waistcoat.

He had performed an act of war.

She gathered up the ashes in two hands and flung them at him. He scooped together some more black, charred bits, and she turned, running for further ammunition. He chased after her. Ashes hit her back.

She squealed, curse him. Like a girl.

Gen found more ashes on the floor and tossed them in his direction, before trying to take shelter behind the remnants of a chair. He plucked the chair out of the way and tossed another dark cloud at her. She threw some back. Their efforts turned into a scrabble. They chased each other over the destroyed kitchens, fistfuls of ash being cast into the air.

At some point, Gen found herself laughing. It was ridiculous, a marquess chasing her about the rubble of her kitchens, hurling ashes at her. She landed a particularly fine shot at him, splattering ash on his snowy, elaborately tied cravat. He growled and charged for her.

With another embarrassingly feminine squeal, Gen turned to run.

Two hands clamped on her waist.

"I've got you now." His low voice sent a shiver of anticipation through her, and it had nothing to do with fear.

He spun her about. Her sole defense was to smear her dirtied hands on his cheeks to stay him from his assault. Which she did, to the peril of her common sense.

Because the moment her hands were upon his skin, she couldn't stop touching him. He was warm, and the connection between them sent a prickle of awareness up her arms, then blossoming, overtaking her. Those sensations landed low in her belly, sending a different heat, like warm honey, trickling to her core.

The levity slowly leached from his face. The dimples disappeared. The air between them burned hotter than any fire. He was going to kiss her. And she was going to welcome it.

Oh, bloody hell.

Who was she fooling?

She was going to kiss him first. And she was going to goddamn love it.

She pulled his face toward hers and rose on her toes. Their lips sealed, and she was lost. His mouth was nothing at all like what she had expected. Warmer, it seemed, than his flesh. Lips full and succulent. Lips she could kiss for days. His fingers tightened on her waist, biting into her tender skin.

And she loved it.

His tongue flicked over the seam of her lips, and she

loved that too. So much that she opened for him. This kiss was nothing like any which had preceded it. He licked into her mouth, claiming her boldly. And he tasted of tea and sugar. The slide of his tongue stole a moan from her.

He moved them as one, guiding her until her back connected with plaster. And then, he settled a firm masculine thigh between her trouser-clad legs. She loved that, as well. Loved it so much, she arched into that intruding limb of his. His thigh was against her most private flesh, the place where she was aching and coming to life.

Aye, she loved it.

Loved it far too much.

She sucked on his tongue and kissed him harder whilst she rode that muscled thigh of his. Sparks began between her thighs and skittered up her spine. Her breasts were aching against their binding, the nipples hard and hungry so that each movement she made, leading to the slightest hint of friction, increased her need.

Of their own accord, her fingers moved, sliding into the thickness of his dark hair. How luxurious and silken-soft his mane was. For a wild moment, she wondered what it would feel like everywhere. On her breasts. Between her legs.

She wasn't supposed to know of such sinful acts. Her brothers had done their damnedest to keep her innocent—first Gavin and then the rest, Dom, Devil, Blade, and Demon. But she was curious. She'd kissed plenty of coves. And she had spent the last few years in a gaming hell. She'd made friends with ladybirds aplenty.

She knew what pleasure a man could give a woman with his tongue. Not in her mouth alone.

But had she not been cured of the desire to experience such wickedness?

No, whispered a seditious voice inside her. *You will never be cured. You're a bastard Winter.*

She should have told that voice to go to the devil, but instead, she kissed the Marquess of Sundenbury with renewed determination. She ran her tongue against his. And she rubbed herself shamelessly against his thigh. Rather in the fashion of a feline desperate to be bred.

An instant, shocking thought of the handsome marquess in her bed, atop her, flashed in her mind. He would kiss her everywhere with that mouth that had been made for sin. And she would love that, too. Very much.

He was a problem, the marquess.

She had always known it, before he had even arrived at her hell. But now he was here, and they were covered in soot, kissing each other frantically in what remained of her kitchens, and…

And she could not even be bothered to care about anything else. He was all there was. Sundenbury, his mouth, his tongue, his strength. Other men tried to intimidate with their size. She had known men who were brutes. Her mother's last protector had been one of those vile sorts. But Sundenbury was simultaneously capable of charming, wooing with his strength, and making her feel wondrously alive.

The problem with the marquess was that she wanted him.

Desperately.

Enough to ask him to bed her in the midst of the day after her kitchens had been set ablaze the night before. After her hopes and dreams, her entire future as the proprietress of Lady Fortune, were all in terrible danger.

He kissed her sinuously, deliciously. The marquess may be a horrible gambler, but he was a tremendous kisser. So tremendous. He did things… *Oh, hell.* She did not know what he did. Her brain was turning to ash, rivaling the heaps surrounding them in the destroyed kitchens.

His hands were on her, moving now. Caressing. Grasping

her bottom, fingers kneading the tender flesh through her trousers, yanking her more firmly against him. And her thigh was rubbing against his cock. There was no question of what part of his anatomy she was brushing against. He was long and thick and hard. Which meant he wanted her. Molly had said that when a man was crazed with lust, his rod swelled and grew stiff, and the only answer for it was a sound frigging.

Curiosity stirred. The same curiosity that had once almost gotten her into so much trouble. But this time, it would not be quelled. She was older and, she hoped, wiser. Her lesson had been learned. There would be no trusting this handsome lord who could not keep from losing every ha'penny his father had ever bestowed upon him. She was beyond being manipulated or easily led astray; she would do what she wanted, as she wished.

Her hands left his hair. She touched him everywhere she could, investigating the breadth of his shoulders, the muscled wall of his chest, the strength of his arms. For a spoiled lord, he was all cord and sinew, delicious for her fingertips to explore. And explore him she did, as she kissed him back with all the desire clamoring within her, begging to be released, to be answered.

That would be a mistake, and she knew it.

More of a mistake than allowing him into her chamber this morning had been. Aye, he had slept on the floor as he had promised, Arthur as his bedfellow, but there were bonds being forged between them. A closeness she could not like.

And still she kissed him, her lips moving hungrily in response to his, her tongue sliding against his. Still, she allowed her head to fall back against the wall when he dragged his mouth down her throat. When he opened his mouth, sucking the flesh, his tongue flicking out to taste her skin, her knees almost went weak.

She clutched his shoulders, attempting to remain upright. This was the distraction she needed from the devastation which had been wrought. Until she became aware of a throat being cleared. Of a discreet cough. Then another, not so discreet.

That sound punched its way through the lusty fog clouding her mind. Her eyes opened, and over Sundenbury's shoulder, she spied Peter. Peter whose jaw was clenched, and who bore the look of a man who was deuced uncomfortable. He was trusted, plucked from The Devil's Spawn, something like an additional brother to her. Protective to a fault. She knew Peter would give his life for hers.

She also knew there had to be a damned good reason for him to linger and dare interrupt her. She braced her palms on the marquess's shoulders and pushed at the same moment she addressed Peter.

"What is it, Peter?" she asked curtly, hating herself for the breathlessness in her voice.

Not the first time since Sundenbury's arrival here in her territory. Ought to make it the last.

For his part, Sundenbury stiffened and straightened, shielding her from Peter's view with his body, as if to protect her modesty. Silly man. She had none.

"Your brothers are here, Gen," Peter said quietly, before disappearing as stealthily as he had arrived.

"Fuck," she swore soundly, shoving harder at Sundenbury's chest. "Some sodding distance, Blunderbury."

If her brothers burst into the kitchens now, with what she and the marquess had been doing clear, she shuddered to think what would happen. Nor would she ever hear the end of it.

Too late.

Dom, Devil, Blade, Demon, and Gav stormed past Peter,

countenances all as stony as if they were about to gut a man with their weapons.

"What the hell has happened?" demanded her eldest brother, Dom.

"And why are you standing so close to Gen, Sundenbury?" growled Devil.

She winced. This little interview was not going to go well.

* * *

HELL.

Of all the times when the burned remnants of a gaming hell's kitchens were invaded by a horde of Winters…

Max would have chuckled at the sheer ludicrousness of such a thought had he not just been kissing the sister of said Winter horde senseless mere moments ago. And were he not currently sporting a cockstand roughly the size of London. Fortunately, the cockstand was subsiding as a result of being pinned beneath the blistering glare of Devil Winter, husband of his sister Evie.

"Miss Winter had soot on her face," he improvised. "I was attempting to aid her in its removal."

Belatedly, he extracted a handkerchief from his waistcoat and held it aloft.

Not particularly convincing.

"Should you not have already had the thing out?" Blade asked. "If it was truly soot you were after, that is."

"Whose idea was it to allow this bloody fop to weasel his way into Lady Fortune, anyhow?" Demon Winter demanded, looking surly. And deadly.

Max took exception to the slur. He stepped forward, chin raised. "I may be many things, but I can assure you I am no fop, Mr. Winter."

Gavin Winter cracked his knuckles. The prizefighter

possessed massive, meaty fists, which had decimated many an opponent. "Fop or not, if you harm a hair on Gen's head, you'll be getting a call from me. And you aren't going to like it, Sundenbury."

He had no intention of harming Gen Winter. All he wanted was to bed her. But he was not about to admit that to these surly Winter men. Some of whom appeared to want to introduce him to their fists at the moment. Even so, he felt strangely powerful. This woman was worth fighting for.

He stepped forward. "I have been threatened and beaten regularly over the last year. I am afraid your threats do not concern me, Mr. Winter."

This did not please Gavin Winter. Not in the slightest.

The prizefighter stalked closer. "They ought to concern you. I can give you a nap with one hand tied behind my bloody back."

Miss Winter dashed in front of him then, her golden hair bound with a thong at her nape that left the rest of the silken locks free to cascade down her back. He regretted not running his fingers through those tempting tresses when he had the chance. Soon, he promised himself.

"Settle yourself, Gav," she warned her brother in a stern, commanding voice. "No one is going to give anyone a nap. No fists, no blades. I've enough on my shoulders without having to worry about two chaps trying to play rooster. Someone set fire to my kitchens last night."

"We know," Dominic Winter said, his expression harsh, his voice hard. "That is why we are all here. No one sets fire to our sister's hell and lives to tell the tale. Whoever was behind this is going to pay."

Max supposed he should not be surprised by the appearance of so many Winters. As the illegitimate faction of the hideously wealthy Winter family who had earned their fortune in trade, they were notoriously protective of each other. Their ranks were tight.

"If anything, you ought to offer Sundenbury your thanks as I have done," Gen was telling her brothers. "If he hadn't heard the breaking glass and come to check upon its source, we may have never noticed there was a fire until it was too late. I was asleep when it happened."

"Right helpful of him," Gavin Winter said, still glaring at Max as if he intended to slide a blade between his ribs at the earliest available opportunity. "Fancy that, a cove hearing breaking glass and rushing to the aid of everyone. A bloody hero, he is."

The sarcasm was not lost upon Max, and nor was it upon Gen. She spoke before Max could defend himself.

"Gav, he did not set it himself," she chastised.

"My aim is to keep from trouble," he added. "I am helping Miss Winter. I would never dream of hurting her or hindering her hell in anyway. I wish to see her succeed."

And he did, with a ferocity that took him by surprise. He could not recall the last time he had been touched so strongly by anything but the need to make his next wager. The desolation in Genevieve Winter's face when he had entered the kitchens earlier—the tears shimmering in her vibrant blue eyes—had cut him as surely as any blade. He hated watching her in pain. Such a strong, proud, capable woman.

He had never admired another more.

"Hmm," was all Gavin Winter said, his expression suggesting he remained decidedly unconvinced by both his sister's and Max's attempts at explanation.

"Did you see anyone last night?" Dominic Winter asked next, steering their dialogue back to the important question of who was responsible for this act of unspeakable destruction.

Max shook his head. "I wish I had. I heard breaking glass.

By the time I realized its source, the kitchens were already ablaze. I roused Peter, so that he could assemble a force to fight the fire, and then I raced to get Miss Winter herself and see to her safety."

Wisely, he refrained from mentioning Miss Winter had been naked before him for a few moments as she donned trousers and shirt. No good could come of such a revelation.

Dom, who was married to Max's other sister, Addy, nodded, his expression still stark and lined with concern. He was a man who cared deeply for his family, but he was also a ruthless man, and an enemy no one would ever wish to make.

Which made one wonder why anyone would dare to attack his sister's gaming hell in such flagrant fashion.

"Who do you think would have set fire to my hell?" Gen asked. "Jasper Sutton, that son of a whore?"

Her language was blistering. Max was going to have to work on that. A future lesson was decidedly in order. Even if the ladies she intended to attract to her gaming hell were of the fast and wild set, which they would need to be, she would have to bring a more polished version of Genevieve Winter to the floor if she wanted to succeed.

And since she hadn't any competition, the odds were decidedly in her favor.

There were women who loved to gamble. Women who embraced all things wicked. *Hell.* He had neglected to ask her if she intended to have entertainments for the ladies at her establishment. The notion of having a cicisbeo or three at the ready for her clientele...

A surge of jealousy that was swift and potent hit him. Jealousy he had no right to feel, he reminded himself. All he had done was kiss her.

Belatedly, he realized the Winters were all discussing the possibilities of which of their enemies would have dared to be so brazen. The Winters and Suttons had been coexisting beneath a tentative truce. Dom Winter did not believe Jasper Sutton, who was the head of the Sutton family, would dare to break that pax. Too much was at stake.

"One of Paul Wilmore's men," Devil suggested. "Setting a blaze to decimate a competitor is just the sort of thing Wilmore would have done. The bastard may be dead, but his men aren't. His brother has been chirping to everyone who'll listen about trying to get his revenge."

Miss Winter nodded. "Aye. Stands to reason it could be one of the Wilmore crew, mayhap the brother. They're the sorts of dirty scoundrels who would do it. But I ain't a competitor. No one else has a hell for ladies. I don't understand."

The Winter brothers exchanged glances, and Max knew what they were thinking. Also, what they did not know how to tell their bold, intelligent, fearless sister.

"It is possible that is the reason for the fire being set," he told her gently. "Someone may take exception to the idea of a club that is exclusively for ladies."

Her head jerked toward him, and he could not help but to take note of the state of her lips, swollen from his kisses. A searing sense of accomplishment burned through him. Along with the desire to do it again. And again.

Soon.

"The hell they would," she said, scowling at him as if he had been the origin of the hatred and the fire and the small-mindedness instead of some nameless, faceless enemy.

Dom Winter raised a brow, sending him a look.

Yes, well. He had rather volunteered himself, had he not?

He cleared his throat. "I am afraid someone would be motivated for such a witless reason, Miss Winter. Or perhaps by a merging of the two—an enemy seeking revenge who is outraged that you are opening a gaming hell for ladies only."

"I will speak with Sutton myself," Dom offered. "I will make certain this is not the work of any of his men. For now, we have brought with us some men who will patrol your perimeter to keep something like this from happening again. We have men to restore the kitchens—"

"No," Miss Winter interrupted, firm. "I will speak with Sutton, and I'll hire my own men to restore the kitchens. I'll accept your patrol until I can hire my own."

Max was not surprised. Miss Genevieve Winter had shown herself to be spectacularly independent.

Her brothers, however, were equally determined to protect her.

"Gen, we are family. Family helps family," Dom Winter said.

"We are and we do," she acknowledged. "But Lady Fortune is something I want to do myself. We've had this talk before."

"Aye," Devil interrupted, looking ominous. "That was before someone attempted to burn down your hell, Gen. You could have been killed."

A small shiver ran through her willowy form, so subtle Max was sure her brothers likely did not see it. But he was near enough, and aware enough of her every move, to take note. What had happened last night had shaken this ordinarily indefatigable woman. Yet she was determined to meet the challenges facing her alone.

Max stepped forward, standing at her side. It was a place that felt natural, right to his marrow. "I am happy to offer my aid to Miss Winter in any capacity."

Dom and Devil stared. Blade Winter looked skeptical. Demon winced. Gavin looked as if he still wanted to plant Max a facer.

"You, Sundenbury?" Dom asked.

He was aware of Miss Winter's regard. Max cocked his

head to the side, and their stares clashed and held. He was not certain what he read in her expression. She remained an enigma to him. However, he swore he saw a hint of something like appreciation.

"Me," he said softly, but he was still not looking at Dom Winter when he said the word.

He was captured by Miss Winter's bright eyes, her soot-streaked beauty. There was a smudge of dirt on the tip of her nose that he longed to wipe clean with his forgotten handkerchief. But not whilst they had an audience of bloodthirsty Winter brothers, he reminded himself.

She nodded. "Thank you, Sundenbury."

No Dunderhead or Blunderbury? His elation was instant and likely foolish. The truth was, he had never worked this hard to woo any woman in his life. He was the heir to a duke. He had been told he was reasonably handsome, and he possessed a looking glass that suggested he was not terrible to gaze upon. True, he did have a reputation as something of a wastrel, and not without cause, but he had never lacked for female companionship.

Suddenly, however, it was not any female companionship he wanted. It was only this one's companionship. And more. Far more.

A foreign emotion swelled in his chest as he nodded. "My pleasure, Miss Winter."

"Someone set fire to your hell, and you are going to rely on Sundenbury but refuse our offer of help?" Gavin demanded, sounding indignant.

Max had to bite his lip to keep from grinning.

"Aye." Miss Winter nodded. "That's the way of it."

He was going to have to kiss Genevieve Winter more often.

CHAPTER 6

"Where are you going?"

Gen jumped, emitting an embarrassing squeal as she waited for her curricle in the rear of Lady Fortune. Hand to her heart, she turned to find the marquess bearing down on her. He was dressed as if he intended to make a call, from his impeccable hat to his shiny boots.

"Damn it, Sundenbury, stop sneaking about like a cracksman searching for the silver in a fancy house while everyone is asleep," she chastised.

In truth, her irritation should have been directed toward herself.

Ever since he had kissed her in the kitchens the day before, she had been on edge. All too aware of the handsome lord. When he was in a room, he seemed to steal all the air from it. When he was not in a room, he clouded her thoughts just as if he were there. She had done her utmost to keep her distance from him after her brothers had finally left.

Last night, he had insisted on sleeping on her floor, but she had refused. Being alone in a room with him was not something she intended to do any time soon. She had far greater concerns on her mind just now. There was a war being waged against her, and she was determined to find out who was behind it and why. Lady Fortune had to come first, before everything and everyone.

That was simply the way of it.

"Forgive me, empress," he said with that easy charm of his and another deadly grin. "It was not my intention to startle you."

His dimples mocked her.

"You didn't startle me," she said with a sniff. Which was a lie, of course. "Sometimes, a woman wants to be alone with her thoughts while she waits for her curricle."

"Understood." He nodded, stopping distressingly near to her. His scent carried to her on the breeze, far more alluring than the ordinary stink of the streets. "Which brings us back to my initial question, the one you failed to answer. Where are you going?"

"Wherever I direct my curricle, Marquess."

Young Davy, who was a pickpocket her brother Dom had taken under his wing in Oxfordshire a year ago, arrived with the curricle, pulling it to a stop. Davy, while still reluctant to curtail his pickpocketing, was keen to learn more. Gen had decided to bring him to Lady Fortune in hopes he would find a role that suited him. Thus far, he had been doing an admirable job of tending to the stables.

"Here you be, miss," Davy called down.

"Thank you, lad." She turned back to the marquess, narrowing her gaze at him. "Where are *you* going?"

The cursed grin deepened. "Wherever you are going, of course."

"No, you aren't." She stepped up into the curricle, accepting the reins from Davy, who brushed against her coat in the process.

He tipped his hat to her as the glint of metal disappeared into his coat.

The little shite.

She caught his arm. "Lad, if you thieve my blade, I'll make you clean the chamber pots for a fortnight."

Davy's horror was reflected on his face as he hastily withdrew the blade and held it out for Gen's retrieval. "Christ. Here you are, miss."

She took it. "Thank you. No more filching, lad."

He had the grace to look shamefaced. "Aye, Miss Winter."

Davy leapt from the curricle with the grace of a cat, but before she could be on her way, someone was taking his place on the box. A tall, wickedly handsome someone.

Was it wrong of her to take a moment to admire the way his trousers molded to his legs as he sat at her side? Was it sinful to take pleasure in his thigh brushing against hers, in the heat he exuded? In his nearness?

Yes.

Also, she did not give a damn.

"What are you doing in my curricle, Sundenbury?" she demanded.

He appeared unaffected by the sharpness in her voice. Instead, he lounged on the box in an indolent pose, as if it were where he belonged. "I told you, I am going wherever you are."

Blast him.

"I am going to see Jasper Sutton," she elaborated reluctantly. "Don't think you are going to be a welcome face there, Marquess."

"My debts to Sutton have been settled, and I am not accompanying you there to play at the tables. I am coming as your escort, should you need protection."

"I don't need protection." She frowned at him. "I have two blades in my coat and another in my boot."

"I would check your boot, were I you. I believe the scamp may have relieved you of that one following your chastisement over the first."

Her frown heightened even as her fingers reached for her boot. "Impossible. I would have felt…" But her fingers found only an empty sheath. She looked around for Davy, but he had already slyly disappeared. "The cadger! It will be chamber pots for him for a bloody month after this."

"You do realize he could cause you any number of problems, should he begin thieving from the ladies at your club," the marquess pointed out.

"Course I do." But she also had a soft spot for the lad. Generally, he was harmless enough. "I'll be keeping him as far away from the ladies as possible. Trust me."

"I have a pistol," Sundenbury announced, patting his coat. "Small enough to tuck into a pocket your scamp could not reach."

It was embarrassing to think she would have been less prepared than the marquess. And that Davy had stolen the blade from her damned boot without her notice, all whilst the smug, handsome man at her side watched. But she was not about to admit any of that aloud to the marquess.

"Trying to prove your worth, are you?" she asked, setting the curricle into motion.

"I thought I did that yesterday."

She shot him a glance, but all she saw was his profile, strong jaw, the aristocratic blade of his nose, and those full, sensual lips. He did not look like a wastrel. He looked like a fine lord. One quite above her station. One she should not be longing for in this moment as he rode with her to confront Jasper Sutton.

Or ever.

"No more talk of the kiss, or I'll reacquaint my fist with

your beak," she warned, before turning her attention back to the road.

"I was not speaking of the kiss," he said. "I was talking about my timely intervention with the fire. But I would be more than happy to discuss the kisses we shared yesterday if you like."

Heat flooded her cheeks. She was grateful for the brim of her own hat, shading her face.

"No," she bit out. "The contrary, Dunderhead."

Silence descended as she navigated the road, nothing but the familiar, jangling of tack and plodding of hooves and rolling wheels.

"Ah," he said after a bit.

Ah?

She sent another look in his direction. "What does that mean?"

"It means I have begun to understand how to translate you, empress." He tilted his head to the side, giving her a rakish grin.

"Translate me?" She jerked her gaze back to the road, grip on the reins tightening. "I am not a strange language to be deciphered."

"That is where you are wrong, my dear. You most certainly are. But I have been more than pleased to study you."

He made the act sound as if it were an amorous one. As if he had been studying her in bed. And then she realized he had been in her chamber. He had also seen her bare-arsed naked the night of the fire. And he had kissed her. The memory of his mouth on hers had her shifting on the box to ease the pulsing ache throbbing to life in her core. This was unacceptable.

She had an interview with Sutton to concentrate on. And

yet, the man at her side was robbing her of the ability to think.

"You are nattering more than a woman," she groused at him, unkindly and she knew it.

"When you are flustered, annoyed, or embarrassed, I am Dunderhead and Blunderbury."

He was correct.

She bit her lip, deciding to ignore him for the remainder of the trip.

An impossibility, that. The Marquess of Sundenbury was a bold, masculine presence at her side. Tempting, too. Depending upon the shifting of the frigid air, she caught more of his scent.

"Am I not right, Miss Winter?" he pressed when she maintained her silence.

"I ain't some witless bird at one of your fine balls, Marquess," she snapped. "Cease calling me Miss Winter."

"Believe me, I would never confuse you with any of the ladies in my acquaintance."

She found herself distressingly jealous of those ladies. She was sure they were legion. Ladies who simpered and preened and flounced about in proper gowns. Ladies who cared about rules and proper speech and smiling and dipping into curtseys and dancing the waltz. Ladies who were nothing like Gen.

She had never wanted to be that sort of female before; she was happy to be exactly who she was. Women born to the rookeries rarely had the opportunities she had. Her brothers had not pressured her to marry but treated her as an equal. She'd never had to earn her living on her back.

"Miss Winter."

She refused to look at him.

"Gen," he persisted.

She glanced toward him reluctantly. Then she wished she

had not done so at all, for his handsome face made an answering pang spark to life within her. "What is it?"

"That was a compliment," he said, smiling and revealing the faintest hint of those dimples she could not seem to resist.

A compliment. She did not receive those terribly often, mostly because Gavin had threatened the teeth of every man in their acquaintance, following what had happened with Gregory. She had not realized how much she had been longing for them. She felt rather like Arthur must have done when she rescued him from the streets, desperately seeking praise, kindness.

Warmth.

She cleared her throat. "Didn't exactly sound like one, Sundenbury."

His smile deepened, and she had to look away from the beauty of it.

"It was, Gen. Believe me. It was."

More of that fatal warmth, blossoming in her belly. More longing. That ache between her thighs would never quite flee.

But Gen kept her attention trained upon the road as they approached the Sutton's hell. She would need to be sharp as any blade for what was to come next.

"Save your compliments," she bit out. "We've arrived at enemy territory."

* * *

JASPER SUTTON WAS A TALL, dark-haired beast of a man seated behind a massive desk with lion heads carved on the legs. Max had met the gaming hell owner on previous occasions. The man walked through the tables of his club like a medieval king presiding over his subjects. And Max had been one such subject, to his shame.

He had spent more time than he cared to recall or admit within this hell's walls, and he had lost more blunt than he had been able to recoup. Sutton had sent men after him who'd had no qualms about delivering a sound trouncing to him. Max counted himself a decent fighter, but when he was outnumbered and attacked from behind, well...

His beating had been thorough.

It felt strange standing within this ruthless man's lair with Genevieve Winter at his side. Mayhap it was truly foolish of him to believe he could defend her. The men guarding Sutton's doors looked as if they were the sort who would happily murder a duke's heir as well as a common thief.

"Gen Winter," Sutton said, rising to his feet from behind his desk, his gaze far too bold for Max's liking as they raked over her form.

"Jasper Sutton," she returned, her dislike for the man apparent in both her tone and her countenance.

"And Lord Sundenbury." Sutton's lips took on a sneer. "Have you come to lose all your blunt at my tables?"

"Clever sally," Max drawled, as if he were unaffected by the jab. "I have come to accompany Miss Winter, lest you act less than the gentleman."

Jasper Sutton's grin was feral. "We all know I ain't a gentleman, don't we? Was born a scourge, and I fully intend to be one when I cock up my toes."

"Worse than a scourge," Gen said at Max's side. "A spider-arsed prick is more like."

Spider-arsed?

Quite inventive, even for her standards. Max had to admit he was both impressed and nonplussed at the oath. For instance, what did it mean? And did he truly wish to know?

Max winced.

"Fine praise coming from a petticoat who pretends to be a cull." Sutton tipped an imaginary hat to her, as if impressed with her insult.

The tension in the room was thicker than molasses.

"I ain't pretending anything, Sutton. I am who I am, and I answer to no man."

"No man, eh?" Sutton raised a brow. "What's the cove doing here, then? Working off his latest debts by bedding the Winter spinster because no one else will?"

Max saw Gen's hand sliding into her waistcoat and decided it was time to attempt civility before she decided to throw a blade at the mocking hell owner before them. He stepped forward, putting himself between Gen and Sutton, in the fashion of a wall.

"You will apologize for the insult to Miss Winter," he told Sutton coolly.

"We've an old feud, her and me," Sutton said, defiant. "I ain't apologizing."

Hell and damnation.

Max did not want to think about what may have been the source of such a feud, but he was willing to wager the dukedom he was set to inherit one day that it had something to do with Sutton lusting after Gen. What man would not? She was beautiful, but it was her daring, wit, and refusal to bend to the world around her that rendered her so much more alluring. Intoxicating, in fact.

He wanted her more than he had ever wanted the next turn of a card.

Which was bloody terrifying, and nothing he could concern himself with in this moment as he faced a scowling Jasper Sutton.

"I do not give a damn what your feud is, Sutton," he said calmly. "You will apologize to Miss Winter."

"This fop speaks for you now, aye?" Sutton prodded Gen.

"Thought you wanted nothing to do with coves, fancy or otherwise."

Gen was at Max's side again, her chin high. "I speak for myself, Sutton. And I never said I wanted nothing to do with coves. I said I wanted nothing to do with *you*."

Ah. He had not been far from the mark with his supposition. That had to sting Sutton. The acknowledgment simultaneously stung and pleased him. Stung him because he did not like to think of her in a situation with another man where she would have cause to rebuff his romantic overtures. Pleased because she had not treated him in the same fashion.

The way she had kissed him back yesterday had been enough to make a man go up in flames. And Max very nearly had done. Such a conflagration would have destroyed what the original fire had not, he had no doubt.

Sutton's jaw tightened, but he showed no other sign of emotion. His countenance was impassive and cold as ever. "Begs the question what you're doing here, then?"

Max held his tongue, allowing Gen to speak, knowing it was not his place. She would likely deliver him a blistering rebuke for leaping to her defense as it was.

"There was a fire in my club," she said. "Last night. Someone broke a window and set my kitchens ablaze."

Sutton nodded. "Aye. I heard about it. Sit."

Sutton ought to have known better than to command Genevieve Winter to do anything. Max almost took pity on the man. His autocratic nature left him sorely unmanned in a battle of wits with her. He was clearly accustomed to everyone fearing him and bowing to his every wish. *Hell*, Max had been on the receiving end of Sutton's mercenaries' fists, so he could well understand why people feared the man.

"I'll not sit," Gen said. "This call will be short. What do you know about the fire?"

Sutton's expression went mulish. "That it was set."

"What else?" she prodded through gritted teeth.

"Nothing," Sutton snapped. "Do you think I did it, Gen?"

Max's protective instincts rose. Why the devil was he being so familiar? Daring to call her Gen? Max had only just allowed himself to think of her in such terms, and that was after his tongue had been in her mouth.

"Tell me you didn't," she challenged, voice cold. Unyielding.

A muscle in Sutton's jaw clenched. "I didn't."

Max stared at the man, wondering if he was trustworthy. Suspecting he was not.

"Have you any word about the fire?" Max ventured. "From outside sources? Heard any rumblings about a woman opening a gaming hell exclusively for ladies? Enemies of the Winters?"

Sutton flashed a grim half smile. "Time was, I was an enemy of the Winters. But we have a truce now, eh, Gen?"

She scowled. "Barely. But you didn't answer his lordship's question. Do you know anything?"

"And if I do?" Sutton cocked his head. "What's in it for me?"

By God, the man was not propositioning Gen—asking her to barter her body for information—before Max, was he? His body moved before his mind comprehended what the rest of him was about. He stormed forward, slapping his palms on the polished lion desk.

"Tell us what you know and I shan't challenge you to a duel, Sutton," he demanded.

Lord knew where the challenge emerged from. It was not the sort Max would have ever issued in his former life. The one where he drank and gambled himself to oblivion without a care in the world. But he was a changed man now.

He was a man who *did* care. One who took notice of rights and wrongs.

One who wanted to be the solution more than he wished to be the problem.

Sutton's countenance shifted, growing more impenetrable. Colder. More ruthless. "Careful, Lord Sundenbury. I might accept that challenge."

"No duels on my behalf," Gen interrupted. "Cease circling each other like a pair of dogs. I came here for answers, Sutton."

"And I may have them, but they come with a price," Sutton said.

"Name it," Gen barked.

"One night with you." Sutton's grin deepened in unabashed enjoyment.

"No," Max bit out before he could stop himself or think better of his reaction. "Go to hell, Sutton."

"In case you haven't taken note, Sundenbury, the East End is hell," snapped Sutton, cocky as ever. "And I'm already here, the devil reigning over it all."

"You don't reign over the East End," Gen was quick to deny. "You are second-in-command to the Winters, and you hate it. Admit it. That is why you set fire to my hell, Jasper, is it not? Or is it because I wouldn't let you into my bed?"

Well, bloody fucking hell.

There it was.

If Max had harbored any doubts, he now had proof that Jasper Sutton had wanted Genevieve Winter in his bed.

Sutton sneered. "I wouldn't set fire to your hell if it were the last hell in the East End. You aren't competition for me. I've a square thing with Dom Winter. I'll not ruin it for a woman no matter how much I want her. And to be fair, love, I don't want you that much. There are plenty more where you came from."

Max wanted to call the bastard out for that alone. There were decidedly not more where Genevieve Winter had come from. Indeed, there was not one other like her. He could damned well guarantee it.

"No need for bitterness over what you cannot have, Sutton," Max said. "Tell us what you know about the fire."

Sutton's narrow glare landed on Max with ominous precision. "Tread with care, Sundenbury."

"Threaten him and you threaten all the Winters," Gen said at his side. "Don't think you want to do that, do you, Sutton?"

Her championing of him sent an unexpected rush through Max. No one had ever defended him before. And certainly never someone like Genevieve Winter. He was not entirely certain he deserved it. *Hell.* He knew he didn't. But he would take it, nonetheless. Shamelessly, too.

"No," Sutton relented, nostrils flaring with displeasure. "Sundenbury is tupping you. I understand. Save your threats, Gen."

Tupping? Max started making his way around the desk, but Gen placed a staying hand on his elbow.

One that said *wait*.

He obeyed, because she was likely correct. And it was likely his protective—and possessive—instincts reacting once more.

"Well, then?" she asked expectantly.

Max could not help but to be impressed by the manner in which she had one of the most feared gaming hell barons in the East End bowing and scraping to her.

Sutton sighed. "Paul Wilmore's brother, Ruben. Look to that rat first. He has been running his mouth, cursing you and your brothers this last year. Some of my men overheard him swearing he was going to bring the Winters to their knees at last, using Lady Fortune as an example. I have been watching him, but only within my hell. Beyond…"

"Beyond is anyone's guess. Fair enough," Gen declared with a nod. "Ruben Wilmore? That is all you have heard?"

Sutton nodded. "I would suspect him before any others."

His tone was grave. Serious. Max believed him, though he was still inclined to take up the cudgels and face the man at dawn.

"Thank you, Jasper," Gen said.

Sutton inclined his head. "You are, as ever, the queen of the East End. The rest of us are but your vassals."

How correct he was in that assessment.

"Damned right you are," Genevieve Winter said, echoing Max's thoughts. "Thank you for the information, Sutton." She turned to Max. "My lord?"

He offered her his arm. And she took it.

Together, they walked from Jasper Sutton's gaming hell.

CHAPTER 7

Gen had a problem much larger than burned kitchens and an enemy out to destroy her gaming hell before it even opened its doors for business.

It was a tall, handsome, man-shaped problem. With dimples.

And said problem was standing before her, bearing a plate of honey cakes.

"I thought you might be hungry," he announced as he deposited them upon her desk with a flourish.

Her stomach growled, for the devastation of the fire, which was currently being repaired by the workmen she had hired, meant she had not breakfasted yet this morning. The plate of cakes looked delicious.

"I am working," she returned, determined to ignore both forms of temptation—marquess and honey cakes.

Gen concentrated on her ledgers. Funds were growing thin thanks to the unexpected expense of reconstructing her kitchens and hiring additional men. She needed to be certain she was leaving herself enough blunt to float the hell.

"Can you not work and eat at the same time?" he asked,

not leaving her in peace as she would have wished but rather skirting her desk and settling his arse upon the corner of it.

"Work first, eat later," she said, refusing to look at him.

Citrus and bay taunted her. Sundenbury's scent. The scent of seduction.

She had restraint. She tallied the Madeira wine she had recently purchased, enough stores to last at least a full month of operation, by her estimation.

"Just one cake?"

She gritted her teeth and pressed too hard on her quill. The nib broke. She threw her pen upon her ledgers and turned her attention to him at last. She wasn't sure which she wanted to devour more, the man or the breakfast he had brought her.

This would not do.

She cocked her head, considering him with what she hoped was a glare instead of a leer. "Why is your arse always on my desk, Marquess?"

"I enjoy vexing you." He grinned.

That was certainly honesty.

She refused to smile back at him. "Because your wits are addled?"

"Because you are beautiful when you are annoyed." His gaze dipped to her lips. "Beautiful when you are not, as well. But there is something about the flash of fire in your eyes, the way your jaw tightens and your chin goes up, that I find utterly irresistible."

Oh.

Irresistible? Her?

Gen wished she had not asked. Because now there was a fluttering sensation in her belly. And longing coursing through her.

"When you are surly, it makes me want to kiss you," he added, voice low with wicked intent.

He was seducing her. It was happening, and she was allowing it.

She found her wits and her voice simultaneously. "I'm too busy for kissing."

He shook his head slowly, pushing off the desk and coming to her. "You should never be too busy for kissing, Gen." His hands found hers, and he pulled her to her feet. "Not ever."

Their fingers were tangled. She should disengage. Punch him in the nose for being so forward. Continue her plan of hiding from him until his month-long sojourn at her gaming hell was at an end. Regain her common sense. Remember that she was Genevieve Winter, and that she had an empire to grow and rule.

But in this moment, all she wanted to do was be the woman holding the Marquess of Sundenbury's hands. She wanted his mouth on hers. Wanted the heat he made her feel, the desire. Wanted to forget about everything and everyone save him.

"It is good to be busy," she said, breathless and hating herself over it. "Being busy keeps me from trouble."

He tugged her closer. Into his lean, strong body. "But there are different sorts of trouble, empress. Good trouble and bad trouble."

She had a feeling the trouble he wanted to embroil her in was the bad variety. The very wicked, sinful, delicious sort.

"There is only one kind of trouble," she argued. "And that is why it must be avoided at all costs."

He brought her ink-stained fingers to his lips, kissing each knuckle one by one. "Generally speaking, I find you to be a wise woman, Genevieve Winter. But on this matter, I regret to inform you that you are decidedly wrong."

No man had ever kissed her knuckles before. The graze of Sundenbury's mouth over her bare skin was incendiary.

She felt it all the way to her toes. Her hands had never seemed extraordinary before. They were useful tools, the means by which she performed any number of tasks. But the Marquess of Sundenbury had just rendered them remarkable. She did not think she could ever look upon her hands again without recalling the brand of his kiss on her knuckles.

"I am not wrong," she forced herself to say. "You are trouble, Marquess. Wicked trouble. Wrong trouble. Distracting trouble. Bloody foolish trouble."

"Good trouble." His grin faded, his countenance going serious. "I want to kiss you again."

Her treacherous heart was racing. Her faithless mouth fairly tingled at the prospect.

She wet her lips. "Kissing is also trouble. I have a hell to open and fire damage to repair and an unknown enemy trying to ruin me and ledgers to balance."

"All those things sound more like trouble." He kissed the knuckles of her other hand, lingering on her thumb, then turned that lovely mouth of his upon her wrist.

The inner part, where she was most sensitive.

She was melting. Gen was sure of it.

"What are you doing?" she demanded.

But there was nothing cutting in her voice. No force. No sense of urgency. Because she did not want him to stop.

"Kissing you." His smile returned, a flash of white, his warm, brown gaze laden with intent. "I want to kiss you everywhere."

She swallowed. "E-everywhere?"

Hell, who was this simpering woman, draping her body against this handsome lord's? She did not recognize herself.

"Everywhere." He kissed her other wrist, then tugged her nearer still, until they were completely aligned, bodies pressed together. He guided her hands to his shoulders and dipped his head to her throat. "Here, on your neck where you are so soft and sensitive." His lips moved over her eager flesh as he spoke. "Here behind your ear." He kissed her there. "On your jaw." There, too. "Your cheek." Kiss. "Nose." Kiss. "And most especially your lips."

"Sundenbury," she whispered, lost in his thrall. Their mouths brushed as she spoke, but still, he did not kiss her there where he had stopped.

"Max," he murmured, rubbing his nose against hers gently.

Gen had never swooned in her life. But she thought she might now.

"Max," she agreed.

"Good empress." And then he rewarded her with the kiss she had been waiting for.

Their mouths sealed. There was only one hunger burning inside her now, and it had nothing to do with the need for sustenance and everything to do with desire for the man holding her close, kissing her with such a delirious blend of tenderness and carnality.

The fingers he had tantalized grasped his coat, pulling him nearer. Desperate to have more of him. He exuded not just heat but something more potent. The thick ridge of him pressed into her belly through the thin layers of their garments. She kissed him back, with more force and intensity than he had expected. He stumbled backward, bringing her with him, into the desk.

There was the sound of something upending. Likely her inkwell. Gen did not care. He was on the desk, and he pulled her atop him so that she was astride his lap, her knees on unforgiving wood. The shift in position had his cockstand pressing against the aching apex of her limbs. She rocked against him, the friction making her moan, sending sparks to her most sensitive parts.

His hands were on her thighs, caressing a path of fire. His

tongue was in her mouth. He tasted sweet, like honey. He must have sampled one of the forgotten cakes. Her fingers sank into his hair, sliding through those soft, dark strands. She kissed him with all the fury and frenzy within. His hands moved to her bottom, squeezing. She rocked on him again, spurred on by his kisses and by overwhelming need burning hot inside her.

She tried to tell herself this was wrong.

That kissing noblemen could only lead to the worst sort of trouble.

That she had a hell to rebuild, a business to start.

So much work to be done, and yet, all she wanted to do was sit in this man's lap and kiss him breathless. He had brought her honey cakes and kissed her knuckles and told her she was beautiful. Likely the actions of a practiced rake. She had not allowed a man past her defenses so thoroughly. Not since Gregory.

This was a mistake. Stupid. Reckless. Foolish.

But somehow, none of that mattered. All that did matter was the marquess. Max. He was nothing as she had supposed he would be. She had not expected teasing grins and dimples and wicked kisses that left her feeling as if her mind were made of pudding.

He groaned into their kiss when she sought more of the friction between their bodies, her cunny riding his cock in such a way that had her feeling as if she would explode like fireworks. She wanted more of that. More of him. More of everything.

He tore his lips from hers, his breathing harsh. "What do you think of that trouble?"

"Stop talking," she bit out, and then she pulled his mouth back to hers.

Their kisses were long and deep. He nipped her lower lip. She returned the favor and he groaned. Their tongues danced. His hands traveled from her bottom to the buttons on her waistcoat, undoing them before he pulled the tails of her shirt from her trousers. And then they were beneath, his knowing fingers working over the bare skin of her stomach. Higher. He cupped her breasts, which she had not bothered to bind that morning, his thumbs rubbing over the straining peaks.

She hummed her approval. His touch was warm and possessive and just…right. They kissed as if the world around them would cease to exist if they stopped. For all she knew, it would. His caresses were exquisite torture. The ache deep within blossomed and spread, twining with desperation.

She had never given herself to a man before, but the realization was there, strong and undeniable, that she wanted to give herself to this one. She shivered at the knowledge and he broke the kiss.

"Are my hands cold?"

"No," she said quickly, fearing he would retreat and not wanting him to, for the moment he stepped away and this madness ended, she would have to resurrect her walls.

This was temporary.

Was it not?

Suddenly, Gen was not sure she wanted it to be.

He drew lazy, tantalizing circles over her nipples. "You are not wearing your binding."

"No." And she was grateful for the omission.

Anything between his hands and her skin seemed a sin of the greatest order.

"It was a dreadful shame, keeping this glory hidden away," he murmured, his lips still in devastating proximity. "But I will admit to a certain selfish satisfaction that you did."

He continued his light massages and teasing, dashing her thoughts to bits. "Satisfaction?"

"I want it to be mine."

His.

The words, the notion, should not have affected her so strongly. A flare of heat in her belly, an aching awareness sparking through the rest of her with the burst of a flash of lightning.

"I do not belong to anyone."

"I don't want to own you, empress." His dark eyes seared hers, reaching deep, finding a need she had not known existed until him. "I want your secrets, the parts of yourself you keep sacred. I want to be the only man who touches you. I want your kisses, your sighs, and your pleasure. I want it all for myself."

How was she to resist?

What if she allowed herself to answer this siren's song? To give herself to him? To accept all the pleasure he offered?

"Yes." Her acquiescence fell from her lips.

"Yes?" He sounded and looked as dazed as she felt.

Was this her, Genevieve Winter, telling a lord, honorific or no, he could have his way with her? Telling the ne'er-do-well duke's heir that he could bed her and have his way with her? That she would give him everything she could give?

She could change her mind now. Tell him his kisses had left her mind hopelessly clouded. It would not be a lie. But there was another truth simmering to the surface, undeniable.

She wanted this man. She wanted him, and she was going to have him. And she was going to give as much of herself as she dared in return.

"Yes," she repeated. "I will be your lover."

* * *

His palms were filled with the luscious weight of Genevieve Winter's breasts. His mouth still burned with the responsive gloriousness of her kiss. She was astride him, on his lap, his cock a scant few layers of fabric from burrowing deep inside the paradise of her cunny.

A wiser man would have accepted her words, tossed her over his shoulder, and hauled her immediately to her bed. But Max had never been particularly good at making wise decisions, as evidenced by the number of times he had played beyond his depths at the green baize and lost everything he had, and then some.

"Lover?" he asked, not liking the word. Wanting to be more to her than someone who shared her body and her bed. Uncertain of what it was he *did* want to be.

Drunk with desire for her.

"I'll not be your mistress, Max. I'm not the sort." She frowned.

He longed to kiss away the furrow of her brow. "What will you be, then?"

"I will be the woman who shares her bed with you until I become the woman who does not."

Somehow, having his hands on her breasts during this discussion felt wrong. He slid his touch lower, settling on her waist. "You are putting an end to us before we have even begun. I do not like it."

"What would you have me say?" She shook her head. "You remain here for another fortnight only. After that, you will return to Mayfair and your balls and your father the duke. You will find yourself a lovely wife and marry and have half a dozen beautiful children and live a perfect life."

He swallowed down a knot of resentment. She was not wrong about the time they had remaining. Nor was she incorrect in supposing his life was meant to be just as she described. One of balls, propriety, courting a suitable lady, wedding her and securing the line with an heir of his own.

But it was not what he wanted. It had never been what he wanted. And the prospect was as unappealing as the notion he would leave Gen in a fortnight's time.

"I could stay longer," he suggested.

"No you can't, Marquess." Her tone was wistful but firm. "This isn't your world."

"It could be."

"I'll give you a fortnight, Max," she said softly. "It is more than I have ever given another, save one."

His jealousy was fierce and instant. "Who?"

She shook her head. "It does not matter. *He* does not matter."

"Did you give yourself to him?" he asked, hating himself for the question, but needing to know.

The manner in which they continued depended upon it. He could either be a tender lover, acquainting her with the newness of lovemaking, or he would be as bold and brash as the intensity of his desire longed for.

She stiffened in his arms, likely misunderstanding the reason for his query. "That is none of your concern."

"Gen." He squeezed her waist gently. "I do not care if you did. I merely need to know whether or not I will be bedding a virgin when the time comes, to save you some pain."

Her cheeks flushed, and her gaze flitted over his shoulder. "Oh. I…yes. You will be bedding a virgin."

If possible, her face went even more scarlet.

Christ, she was beautiful. Her discomfiture was enchanting. He would not have believed she had it in her to be embarrassed. It imbued her with a vulnerability which had been heretofore absent.

"I will take care with you," he said softly, heart thudding

at the knowledge of how completely she was entrusting herself to him. "I promise, Gen."

She nodded, catching her lower lip in her teeth. "I know you will. That is why I chose you."

That is why I chose you.

Her confidence in him astounded.

All his life, he had been a source of disappointment, from leading strings on up. He was not the heir his father had wanted. He was not worthy of the title. He gambled too much, read too little. He was profligate, a scoundrel, a rogue. He was at home with the demimonde rather than the aristocrats with whom he was meant to play. He drank until he was disguised. He lost more money than he had. He embarrassed the vaunted Saltisford legacy.

Oh, he had never lacked in female attention. Women had chosen him to be their lover, their protector, their bed partner for the night. But no one had ever chosen him in the sense that Genevieve Winter had just proclaimed. She was giving him the most precious gift, one which was rare and coveted and one no other had received.

Herself.

He felt like a tarnished necklace of paste gems in comparison.

"You pay me great honor," he told her, attempting to give voice to the tumult reigning within him. Desire, need, awe, and something else.

Something too complicated and potent for him to examine just now.

"You make it sound as if I've just given you a fortune in jewels," she quipped lightly in an obvious attempt to shift the tone.

She was still on his lap, and he was still on fire for her. He gave her waist a gentle squeeze of reassurance. "More than that."

Her lips pursed. "Eh, you may change your mind when the time comes. What if I disappoint?"

He almost laughed at the sheer lunacy of such a question. But he saw that she was serious, so he did not.

"Impossible, empress. You could never disappoint me."

She cocked her head, considering him in a way that made him want to look away, fearful she would see inside him, to a place he did not even know existed. That she would see more of him than he knew himself.

"You aren't at all the man I thought you were, Marquess."

"Max," he reminded her, needing his name on her lips as much as he needed her kiss.

"Max." Her face softened.

On any other woman, he would have said he spied some tenderness in her countenance. But this was Gen Winter, and she was not tender. She was surly and bold and stubborn and unrelenting and so bloody brave, she never failed to take his breath.

"Yes." He kissed her again.

The meeting of their mouths began slowly this time. He wanted to savor her, to leave her with a taste of what awaited her this evening without overwhelming. He could not take a virgin on a desk. He would pay homage to her tonight, in her bed. Her arms twined around his neck, and she tilted her head, kissing him back.

Someone had taught her to kiss.

And mayhap that same someone had broken her heart.

Whoever the bastard was, his loss was Max's gain.

"Now?" she asked against his lips, breathless.

He was so mindless with need for her that it took his befuddled mind a moment to realize the meaning of her inquiry.

He shook his head. "You've work to do, and so have I. Besides, I cannot take a virgin on a desk."

She tortured them both by shifting, rubbing herself over his still painfully erect cock. "Why can't you?"

Damnation.

She was going to be the death of him.

He had not anticipated either the sweetness of her capitulation or the temptation.

He kissed her again, swiftly this time. "I want your first time to be special, Gen. I want to take my time. To kiss and taste every part of you. To make you come apart, until you cannot think or speak because you are so sated."

Her lips parted. "Cocky cove, aren't you?"

There was so much he could say. Max just grinned at her. "Decide if I have reason to be later."

"I don't want to wait."

Unless he was mistaken, Genevieve Winter was pouting. *Splendid.* He wanted her desperate. He wanted her aching for him.

"I believe I knocked over your inkwell earlier," he pointed out in an attempt at distracting her. "We would have to make love in a puddle of ink."

Indeed, it was probably already staining his own arse. His trousers did feel a bit...damp.

"Surely men and women have made love in worse conditions," she countered. "Molly said she once frigged a sailor against a brick building. Said it bit her arse to pieces, but it was worth every moment."

This woman.

"Who the devil is Molly?" Dare he ask?

"One of the bawds at The Devil's Spawn. A right fountain of information for the curious." Gen grinned, unrepentant.

The curious.

He growled. "From this moment on, I shall answer your curiosity. Understood? No bawds giving up their secrets, no other men. I want you to myself."

"For tonight." Her brows rose. "What if I ain't impressed, Sundenbury? I'll not promise you a fortnight until I have something to judge you on."

"I will make certain you are impressed, empress," he vowed. "I will make certain you are very, very, very impressed."

One of his few talents was in his tongue. It was long and dexterous.

"Do not make promises unless you intend to keep them," she drawled.

He slid his hands back to her delicious rump, filling his palms. "I have never intended to keep another promise more, my dear."

A sudden knock on her office door had the effect of a storm cloud breaking open overhead and deluging them. She leapt from his lap and attempted to straighten her shirt, tucking it back into her trousers before buttoning her waistcoat. He rose as well, brushing the wrinkles from his trousers.

"Who's there?" she called.

"Peter. I'm afraid we've a problem, Gen. Our Madeira has been stolen."

More attempts at sabotage? Max's stomach drew into a knot. He had been hoping they would discover who had lit the fire before any more damage was done to either Gen or Lady Fortune.

"Goddamn it," she bit out.

Max winced. "We truly do need to commence a lesson on language."

"Fuck your lessons." She was grim. "I've got bigger problems."

He could not argue the point.

CHAPTER 8

When she was helpless or nervous, Gen liked to perform useful, menial tasks. And tonight, she was both, more than she had ever been before. Because an unknown foe was doing everything in his power to make certain Lady Fortune failed before it had a chance to succeed. And because she had invited the Marquess of Sundenbury into her bed.

She sat by a brace of candles in her private apartment above the gaming hell, penknife in hand as she sharpened the nib of what must have been her tenth quill. In her agitation, she had scavenged all the pens she could find, intent upon doing something useful. Anything to take her mind off the troubling incidents which had befallen Lady Fortune. And anything to keep her from thinking about the marquess's promise.

I will make certain you are very, very, very impressed.

The memory of his low, delicious voice uttering those sinful words to her still sent a shiver down her spine. *Christ and all the saints.* What was she going to do with such a man? How was she going to keep herself from turning into a quivering, stuttering fool? She had already admitted she was a virgin to him.

Grumbling a curse, she worked on the nib in her hands, cutting at a precise angle.

Her entire store of Madeira had been thieved. Gone without a hint of when it may have been taken. None of the details she had hired had seen anyone suspicious lingering about Lady Fortune or entering or leaving. Peter had been conducting a check of the cellar when he had noticed the wine missing.

And after she had finished tallying her ledgers—and tidying the mess of her spilled inkwell—she had confirmed her fears. There were not funds remaining for a replacement store of Madeira. Not if she intended to pay her employees their wages and continue repairing the kitchens, both of which were utter necessities. Gen believed in loyalty and fairness above all else. She wanted everyone in her employ to believe in her, in Lady Fortune, and she wanted them to know they could be assured of the coin she promised them and the bread they needed to put upon their tables.

Damn whoever was attempting to destroy her business to hell. She had sent word of the stolen wine to Dom. Reluctantly, but she had done it. She did not possess the connections in their world that her older brother did. If it was truly Ruben Wilmore behind the attempts to hurt Lady Fortune, Dom would know better than anyone.

But that would do nothing to replenish her Madeira. Oh, she had no doubt that Dom would be more than eager to send her all the wine he possessed at The Devil's Spawn in an effort to aid her. That was the way of things with her siblings. Yet, she balked at asking for or accepting his help. Lady Fortune was meant to be hers, and that meant its battles were hers to fight as well. She would simply have to serve a different drink to her ladies until she had the coin for more Madeira.

She heaved a sigh of irritation at the thought. If she wanted to attract the wealthiest ladies with the most blunt to lose, and if she wanted to make them believe her establishment was exclusive and sought after, she needed Madeira, curse it. She also needed kitchens which were not partially rebuilt and a French chef who was not furious his space had been destroyed.

A sudden tap at the door, almost so light she failed to hear it, had her jumping. The blade of her penknife slipped, slicing into the tender pad of her thumb. On a yowl of pure frustration and pain, she stuffed the digit into her mouth, sucking. The coppery tang of blood met her tongue.

Her door flew open, and the Marquess of Sundenbury came storming across the threshold, looking as if he were charging into battle. He slowed when he spied her and exhaled loudly.

"You are uninjured?" he demanded.

She plucked her thumb from between her lips. "Injured, but the fault is mine. Do close the door before everyone beneath this roof is aware that you are in my chamber."

He retraced his steps and closed the door as she asked before turning and stalking toward her, his countenance still stark. "I was in your chamber before."

"It was after a fire. No one took note," she said, glancing at her thumb and dismayed to find blood oozing steadily from the cut she had given herself.

She was instantly dizzied. The room was spinning.

"Damnation, Gen!" He was on his knees before her in an instant, taking her hand in his. "What the devil happened?"

She glanced back at her thumb, which proved a mistake. Her skin went hot, then cold. Her stomach clenched. "I cut myself."

"You are pale." He pulled a handkerchief from his pocket and wrapped the snowy linen around her thumb, holding it tight.

"The sight of my blood makes me...ill," she managed.

She was lightheaded. On the edge of vomiting. Damn these old wounds, which never seemed to heal. Which took her back to that long-ago day, when Gav had saved her life.

"Take a deep breath," he said, keeping his handkerchief in place. "I will tend to your wound."

She closed her eyes, but the memories were there. The monsters, too. So she opened her eyes, staring at the marquess.

"Breathe, Gen." His gold-brown stare bored into hers, calming, tender.

A reminder she was in the present and the past could not harm her.

She took a gulp of air. She had tattooed her family and others with impunity, the needle she used to implant the pigments in their skin often drawing blood. It was only her own blood that made her ill, the painful reminder of her vulnerability. Of her inability to protect herself from harm.

"Your color is returning." He was calm, reassuring.

A bastion of comfort.

How strange this man she had believed careless and foolish should turn out to be one of the most caring she had ever met, aside from her brothers.

She inhaled again, her pounding heart calming. The past was gone. Her mother was gone. This blood was not the same.

She ran her tongue over her dry lips. "Thank you."

"Of course. I will need to clean the wound for you and bandage it."

"It's scarcely a wound," she forced herself to say, summoning her courage. "A scratch, nothing more."

"Your reaction suggests otherwise," he observed, frowning.

"My reaction was deceiving." She hesitated, not wanting to reveal the truth to him. "It was because of something that happened to me when I was a girl."

That she could speak of the event, describe it in such benign terms, surprised her. But there was no other way to admit her mother had tried to kill her, was there?

"You need not tell me, Gen." His tone was tender.

He was holding her hand, careful to keep the handkerchief wrapped around her thumb, which had begun to throb now that some of her anxiety had subsided. And she realized she wanted to tell him. Not just because he would likely see her scar, but because she trusted him.

"I was stabbed," she blurted. "My brother Gavin saved me. The fear is an old one, the scar long healed. But the memory remains, and whenever I see my own blood, I am taken back to that day."

His expression shifted, hardening. "Christ. You were stabbed when you were a girl? What kind of a monster would harm a child?"

She managed a sad smile. "My mother. She was out of her head. Too much blue ruin, and she had the pox. Thought I was a demon, and she was going to rid herself of me. Gavin heard me scream... I had been running, trying to escape, and she was after my throat."

The fear returned, tightening in her chest. But it was not as heightened as it had been at the sight of her blood.

"My God."

She searched his countenance, thinking he would be appalled to know her own mother had tried to kill her. "You see what stock I come from. I'm tainted. Not just a bastard. Worse."

"You are not responsible for your mother's sins," he said softly.

With a pang, it occurred to her that this was the first time anyone had ever told her those words. And how miraculous they seemed. How hopeful.

She shook her head. "That is not the way of it in this world."

"It damn well should be," he bit out. "You were an innocent child. The woman who should have been protecting you betrayed you."

"Gav was there. He protected me."

"And thank God for that." With an air that was almost worshipful, he raised her hands to his lips for a kiss. "Little wonder you are so strong."

Despite his praise, she was embarrassed, both by her carelessness in cutting herself and her reaction to the blood. "I am not strong, or I would be able to look at a scratch on my thumb without swooning."

"You are wrong, empress." He was serious, no sign of the dimples that tempted and taunted her and yet as alluring as ever. "You are the strongest woman I know. I admire you. Hell, I wish I possessed a crumb of your bravery."

His frank admiration had her cheeks going hot. "You saved us from the fire. That was brave."

"It was necessary." He squeezed her hands gently. "May I unwrap it and see that your wound is properly cleansed?"

She eyed him. "Why are you so determined to take care of me, Marquess?"

No man before him had been so concerned over her. And yet, Max was bringing her honey cakes, accompanying her as she faced Jasper Sutton, fretting over her wounded thumb and her past.

"I care about you," he said simply.

As if he had not just made such a shocking revelation.

As if he had not stolen her ability to speak, this time for an entirely different reason.

She cleared her throat. "You can't care for someone like me."

"There you are wrong, my dear." He tied the handkerchief around her finger before releasing her hands. "I cannot do anything but care for you. All you have to do is let me."

His words were dangerous. So, too, the longing he sparked deep within her. One she had never previously known existed. To be the sort of lady he could court. Hell, to be a lady. To be someone who had been born on the right side of the blanket, in the right part of London. His equal. Someone he might marry.

Good God.

Marriage?

Now her wits were just as addled as her mother's had been.

He rose to his feet, towering over her.

"You needn't charm me, you know," she said, pleased with herself for the coolness in her voice as she stood as well, the lightheadedness she had been experiencing passed. "I have already agreed to allow you to bed me."

"Do not."

"Do not what?" she demanded, searching his gaze.

She wanted to hold him close and kiss him. But she also wanted to send him away. She wanted to guard this other vulnerability within her, the one he had somehow discovered and brought to life.

"Do not make what is between us into something tawdry and sordid," he said. "This is far more than that, and you know it."

It was, and the knowledge terrified her.

His kindness battered down the walls around her heart.

His concern and caring were like balms to all the most ragged, worn places deep within.

"This is a fortnight of pleasure," she denied. "Nothing more. Then, you return to your world and I stay in mine."

His jaw went rigid. "If that is what you wish."

"It is what must be." The reminder was for herself as much as it was for him. "Future dukes and bastard daughters do not mingle in London beyond these walls."

"As you like. Allow me to see your thumb now, if you please."

His bland reaction and change of subject took her by surprise. And disappointed her, if she were brutally honest. But what had she expected? That he would fight? Declare his undying devotion to her?

Foolish, Gen. You have a business to run.

She extended her hand, and he took it once more.

"Close your eyes, empress."

It was still too soon.

She shook her head. "I prefer to leave them open."

He nodded, seeming to understand. "Then look over my shoulder while I loosen the handkerchief."

Gen did as he asked, concentrating her attention upon an irregularity in the wallcoverings at his back. She ought to see something hung there, she thought. One of her drawings, mayhap. And then she thought of drawing the man before her, the one who was tentatively loosening the makeshift bandage on her injured thumb. She hadn't had the time to draw these last few months as she had thrown herself into the preparations for Lady Fortune.

"Hmm."

His low hum almost had her glancing back at him.

She tensed. "What is it?"

"The bleeding has stopped, I believe. The wound does not

appear terribly deep. Fingers, it would seem, are like noses. A great deal of blood initially."

Relief washed over her, along with guilt as she thought of the day she had punched him in the nose. How could she have known just how thoroughly everything between them would change?

"Then we can commence with the night's entertainment. I hadn't expected you this early," she confessed.

In truth, she had not known what to expect at all. The Marquess of Sundenbury was her first assignation.

"I was eager."

His quiet admission stole her attention back. But she did not look at her thumb. Nor at the square of linen she assumed to be marred with the red of her blood. Instead, she looked at his beautiful face.

"As was I," she admitted.

"But after you have wounded yourself, I would not—"

"Max," she interrupted, not wishing to hear the rest of his words.

He raised a brow. "Gen?"

"Kiss me."

He grinned. "With pleasure."

She had a fleeting impression of his dimples and knew a quickening in her heart before his mouth found hers.

* * *

MAX WARNED himself to be gentle. To give as much as he took. She was an innocent, and she had been through a hell the likes of which he could not fathom. Little wonder she had built a fortress around herself. Desperation had struck him, along with fear, when he had opened the door to find her bleeding and pale. With the attacks on Lady Fortune, he had initially been terrified someone had been hiding in her apartments and gone after her. But then he had taken note of the penknife and quills, and the truth had been apparent.

His heart had been pounding ever since his entry at finding her pale and unlike herself. Now, it was pounding for a different reason entirely. Her vulnerability had rendered her even more tempting—the knowledge she trusted him with this dark, painful secret made him feel as if he were the most powerful man in London.

And as his lips moved over hers, all his good intentions fled. The gentleman within disappeared. The fires of need licked into roaring, raging flames, and he was powerless to do anything other than surrender to them.

To *her*.

He kissed Gen softly, deeply, taking his time to torture them. She clutched at his shoulders, offering herself up to him completely. He was going to take everything she had to give. Because everything about Genevieve Winter felt inherently right. Felt as if she were his. As if she always had been, but he had been traveling through life, waiting for the moment when all would weld together and make sense in the form of this brash, beautiful woman.

This night would not be enough. He knew instinctively that no amount of nights would. He wanted more from her than the fortnight she had promised. He was greedy when it came to her.

So greedy, he slid his tongue into her mouth, tasting her. She was sweet like honey yet infinitely more delicious. And she sucked on his tongue with abandon, making the most decadent sound of frustrated pleasure in her throat. That mewl coiled around him, settled deep. Her scent, like a garden bursting into vibrant blossom, left him drunk with passion. His every sense was sharp and painfully aware.

He dared to caress her, learning her curves and lines with his hands, the fabric of her masculine garb keeping him from the prize he sought—all that silken, feminine flesh. He started at her waist, and then he traveled up her back. She was so delicate beneath her jacket, so much more fragile than she seemed, and he felt like this was a side of her only he was privileged to see and know.

The brash, bold, fearless Genevieve Winter.

His.

He tore his mouth from hers, kissing along her jaw, down her throat to where her linen cravat kept him from her skin. Kissed his way to her ear, traced the shell with his lips, absorbed her shiver.

"I want to bring you so much pleasure, you forget how to think," he told her softly. "I want to taste you everywhere."

"You're a rogue, Marquess." Her voice was husky, with a rare undercurrent of teasing.

"Max," he reminded her. "No formality. No boundaries. Nothing between us tonight."

Which reminded him. Too many layers were in the way. He nibbled on the part of her throat available to him as his fingers freed the buttons on her coat from their moorings. She swallowed hard as he slid his hands inside, over her waistcoat; he felt the sudden movement in her neck, the racing of her pulse.

"Max," she whispered, her hands were moving, too. "I want your coat off."

His cockstand was instant.

Slowly, you dolt, he warned himself.

He nuzzled the hollow behind her ear. "I propose an even exchange, empress. For every garment you shed, I shall also remove one article of clothing."

She shrugged her coat to the floor.

There was his lioness.

"Off," she repeated, working on his own buttons.

"Impatient," he said, smiling.

"Eager," she corrected, refusing to allow him the last word, even in their lovemaking.

Had he imagined any different? Of course not. Gen Winter was a woman unlike any other, and that was what made her so bloody special.

Together, they removed his coat, and then it was time to work on cravats. Those knots proved more difficult to undo whilst kissing, resulting in some laughter, then more heated kisses when the knots were at last unraveled.

Her waistcoat was next. He could not resist taking her mouth again as his hands coasted over the swells of her breasts, barely kept confined by the garment. It was erotic as hell, her curves contained by masculine garb, and in a way he had never previously imagined or considered.

Soon, their waistcoats were both gone. She raked her nails over his chest, scoring his nipples, and he palmed her breasts through the cambric of her shirt. They were perfect weights in his hands. Soon, he would have them bare and the anticipation was stoking the fires of his desire into greater heights than before.

There were buttons at the neck, and he plucked them open with a haste that rendered his fingers clumsy. But he felt no embarrassment. Tonight, he was not the practiced seducer. He was merely a man making love to the most magnificent woman he had ever beheld.

Her fingers were similarly plagued as she worked on his shirt.

"You are trembling," he noted against her mouth, reluctant to end their kiss. "Not with fear, I hope."

"Never fear. Not with you."

Had he thought he felt like the most powerful man in London before? Strike that. For now, it was the most powerful man in England. She made him feel like a king instead of a prodigal duke's heir.

"Good." He kissed the corner of her mouth.

The last of the three buttons on her shirt was undone. Reluctantly, he pried his mouth from hers, gazing down at her. Although her golden hair was still trapped in a chignon at her nape, the rest of her looked wild. Lips stained the same color as crushed cherries, full and swollen from his kisses. Eyes pools of blue fire, the obsidian discs of her pupils wide. Her pale throat was marked pink from where he had kissed, licked, and sucked.

Beautiful was not a word sufficient enough to describe her. Nor was breathtaking.

"You are staring," she observed solemnly.

"I am savoring," he countered.

"Savoring me?"

Did she not see herself? Did she not know how incredible she was?

He pressed his forehead to hers.

"You," he affirmed.

"Charming rogue," she said softly, without heat. "I like the way you make me feel."

Her concession took him by surprise. This was yet another new side to her, one he had not imagined existed. He was heartened. And grateful. Humbled, too.

"Once more an even exchange, empress." He rubbed his nose along hers. "I like the way you make me feel also."

"You do?"

"Yes."

This time, she took the initiative, rising on her toes to seal her lips to his once more. They kissed slowly, deeply, tongues meeting. They were both breathless by the time it came to an end, clinging to each other. The passion between them was as raw and hot as it had ever been, about to set the room on fire.

"Why are you still wearing your shirt?" she asked.

Why indeed?

He grasped two fistfuls and hauled it over his head. "Better?"

"Much." Her bright-blue eyes traveled over his chest with the impact of a caress.

His cock twitched as she looked her fill, and when her gaze slipped to the placket of his trousers… Well, he could not contain his enthusiasm. But he need not have feared she would shy away from his obvious reaction to her with maidenly horror. Oh, no. Not Genevieve Winter.

Instead, she reached for him, cupping him through his trousers. And he, helpless beast that he was, groaned, aching for her. Thrust his hips, sending him into her palm with shameless disregard for the fact that she had never allowed a man into her bed before.

"Bloody hell," she said, eyes wide.

He echoed the sentiment wholeheartedly. It required the summoning of all his restraint to keep from spending in his trousers like a green lad who had just seen his first pair of bubbies. That was how strong, how intense her effect was upon him.

"Shall we stop?" he asked, because some shred of the gentleman remained within him, and because he cared for this woman. More than he cared to admit even to himself.

He would not hurt her. Nor would he pressure her into making a decision she would later regret.

She grinned. "Only if you want another punch in the beak, Marquess."

He laughed, relief coursing through him. "I fear it cannot withstand another."

"Wise decision."

Bloody hell, he wanted her so much, his teeth ached. He had never been so at ease with a woman. Nor had he ever experienced this range of emotion—desire so potent he almost melted, then laughter, teasing, gentleness, poignancy and sadness, too. Everything, wrapped up into one mercurial package.

He trailed his forefinger along the gaping vee of her shirt. "I want this off," he said, repeating her earlier words to him.

And just as he had done, she grasped her shirt and pulled it over her head. The action meant she removed her touch from his cock, but he was grateful for the reprieve.

He had touched her earlier in the day, but the beauty of her body had been denied him, concealed as it had been beneath her layers. Now, he could drink in the sight of her. Pale curves, breasts the perfect handfuls and tipped with pink, hard nipples that called for his mouth.

And there, on her abdomen, the most beautiful part of all —the evidence of the horrible tale she had told him earlier. A scar, one long slash healed over in mottled pink flesh, uneven and dark in its contrast to the otherwise smooth creaminess of her skin.

She stood stiffly, shoulders back, rather reminiscent of how he imagined a soldier might look when preparing to charge into battle. But she made no effort to cover the scar or herself.

"Ugly, isn't it?" Her voice cut through the hushed quiet of the room, shaking him from his thoughts.

"No." He shook his head. "Christ no, empress. It is beautiful. *You* are beautiful. A warrior in every sense."

"Just the bastard daughter of a whore and a tradesman with more wealth than honor." Her smile was wry, her voice bitter.

Was that how she thought of herself? *Damnation.* He would have to do everything in his power to disabuse her of such a wrongheaded notion.

"Never speak of yourself in such a fashion again, Gen." He dropped to his knees before her, his lips finding the raised flesh of her scar. He kissed her there. "You are glorious."

"Max," she protested, her hands settling on his shoulders. "I have already told you that I do not require more of your wooing or charm. I have already agreed to share my bed with you."

"I am not wooing or charming." He kissed higher, to where the jagged wound had ended, at her side. "I am being honest. You astound me and humble me and make me wild with wanting you. I admire you more than I can convey with words."

But he would make amends for that lack.

He would show her with his body. He would bring her such pleasure she would never again doubt her worth.

Her fingertips dug into his muscles. "You say everything I want to hear."

"Wrong," he said tenderly, gazing up at her as he caressed her waist and kissed back down her scar. "I say everything you *need* to hear. It is true, Gen. You are bold and intelligent and brave. You have overcome more than I can imagine to be where you are, and in a world dominated by men, you are daring to rule your own kingdom."

"Fine job I am doing of it." She let out a bitter laugh. "I haven't opened yet, and already, I'm in desperate straits."

"We will discover who is behind these cravenly attacks on you and your business," he vowed. "One way or another. But that is for another day. Tonight is about pleasure." He kissed lower, his fingers working the fall of her trousers. "Your complete and absolute pleasure. I am yours to command tonight, empress. Tell me what you want."

He looked up at her and their gazes clashed and held. Her lips were parted, eyes glazed. She wanted this every bit as much as he did. It would seem they were at each other's mercies now.

"I want…" she began, then allowed her words to trail off. "Damn it. I do not know, Max. Show me everything. Do what you wish with me. All I want is you."

He was unprepared for the ferocity of his reaction to those words. Desire flooded him. For a moment, he could not speak.

"Naked," he finally managed. "I want you stripped bare for me."

"Yes," she whispered.

And he stood back, giving her the power once more. Allowing her to make the decisions. She disrobed with surprising haste and finesse. Trousers gone. Stockings gone. He guided her to the chair she had vacated, and she sat.

Max allowed himself a moment to admire her—the turn of her ankles, the elegance of her calves, the fullness of her thighs. The patch of golden curls at the apex of her thighs. *Christ*, even the arches of her feet and her toes were worthy of admiration. She was smooth and feminine and bold.

Mine.

There was that voice again, rising from deep within.

He could not seem to contain it. His need for her was bigger than he was, consuming him, taking control. He sank to the floor before her once more, ready to worship her.

"Show yourself to me," he said. "Please."

He would beg if he needed to. Fortunately, he did not.

She did as he asked. Her knees, which had been pressed together in maidenly shyness, moved apart with painstaking, delicious slowness. And then, all at once, she was revealed. Pink, glistening flesh. Perfection.

He could not wait another moment. His palms traveled over her inner thighs in a caress that left him feeling as if she had branded him. Such softness. Such femininity. So many secrets she hid beneath her trousers and waistcoats and aloof demeanor. He wanted to be the only one who knew them, the one who unlocked each, one by one, the one who kept them forever.

But he did not have forever.

For now, he had tonight.

And for tonight, he would savor.

He slid his touch higher, gliding over her skin, getting nearer to her center, the warmth radiating from her core enough to make him want to hurry in spite of his intentions to the contrary. His questing hands trembled with the force of his ardor as he eased her thighs farther apart.

He dipped his head, pressing a kiss to her inner knee. Then up the same path he had just caressed. Torturing the both of them as he kissed all the way to the swollen bud at the center of her wet heat. He flicked his tongue over her, testing, teasing, tasting.

A guttural oath tore from her, and he would have smiled had he not been so overwhelmed by his own body's reaction to hers. His heart was pounding, his ballocks drawn tight, every part of him aflame. He swirled his tongue, then pulsed, delivering fluttering, light licks to her pearl.

Her fingers threaded through his hair, grasping, tightening. Showing him she liked what he did. He sucked, the musky sweetness of her on his tongue, filling him with more need. He had never tasted anything better. She was ruining him, and he did not care. She was all he wanted.

And he showed her.

Showed her with his lips and teeth. Showed her so thoroughly, she was bucking against him, tugging at his hair, thrusting into his face. And then she was coming apart splendidly. She cried out his name, quaking beneath his mouth as she spent. He gave her no quarter, showed no mercy. Max wanted everything she had to give and then more. He wanted this night, his touch, the pleasure he gave her, to be imprinted upon her memory as thoroughly and irreversibly as ink on paper.

Which was why he did not stop.

As she rocked beneath him, her breaths emerging as ragged pants, he remained where he was, on his knees before her, worshiping her as thoroughly as he could. When he found a place where she was particularly sensitive—the breath hissing from between her lips and a moan echoing through the room—he worked harder. Licked and sucked and nibbled.

"Oh, Max."

Yes, love, he would have told her had not his mouth been blissfully occupied with wringing as much bliss from her as he could. In lieu of that, he nibbled on her pearl until she came a second time, her body undulating beneath his ministrations, her moan the best compliment he had ever been paid.

Genevieve Winter was not a woman who lowered her walls with ease. Nor was she a woman who entrusted herself to others. The honor she gave him was tremendous, and he intended to repay her in every way he could. He licked down her seam, finding her entrance, and tongued her lightly there, where he would claim her soon enough.

Not soon enough according to his body's reaction. He was nearly out of his mind with desire. With need. With her. He could never have enough. To the devil with a fortnight and her nonsensical notion of ending this before they had even begun. He wanted more. He had to have more. The pounding of his heart was proof of the effect she had on him, growing louder by the moment.

"Max."

It took him a moment to realize the sounds were external. Not his heart after all, though that cursed organ was pumping steadily enough.

Rather, the rapid hammering interrupting the silence was the bloody door.

And bloody Peter.

"Gen, we've a problem."

Damnation.

"Max, we must stop," she whispered, sounding frantic.

He settled back on his heels, releasing her with greatest reluctance. "That man has the devil's own timing."

Her cheeks were flushed, eyes bright. She had never been lovelier. She looked thoroughly loved, but he had not loved her nearly well enough this night. There was so much he had to show her. His painfully rigid cock was terrible evidence of that.

"A moment, Peter," she called loudly so that her voice would carry to the man waiting in the hall. But her eyes were on Max's, lingering. Her voice was hushed, then, whispering an apology. "I must see what is wrong."

Yes, she needed to.

He understood.

That did not mean the bitter sting of disappointment did not lance him.

He inclined his head and rose to his feet. "Of course."

"It can't wait," called Peter from the other side of the door.

Max bit back a curse and spun on his heel, collecting his garments in hasty motions.

"I am coming," she returned to Peter.

Not in the bloody way she ought to have been, Max thought grimly. This was meant to be a night devoted to her. A night of nothing but passion. A night where she forgot about all her duties and was allowed to simply be a woman. He wanted to rail against the injustice of this interruption, against whoever was perpetrating these evils upon her establishment. It was not fair.

They dressed in silence, the only sound between them the mutual, hasty rustling of linen. As he stuffed his arms into the sleeves of his coat, she surprised him by laying a hand on his back.

"You are angry?"

He turned to her. She was dressed and deliciously ruffled. Anyone could take one look at her and see plainly what they had been about. He knew a ridiculous surge of pride at that. But little good it did him, for neither of them had gotten what they wanted this night.

He sighed. "I am angry, yes. But not with you, Gen. With the circumstances."

"Lady Fortune must come first," she said, almost apologetically.

Peter pounded on the portal. "Gen? A cracksman's run off with more. Need you out 'ere."

"Damn it," she bit out, echoing the sentiment in Max's heart.

But then she started for the door, leaving him behind.

He was nearly fully dressed. "Wait for me. I'll accompany you."

She turned back, her expression knotted with worry, uncertainty. "It's best if I go on my own."

Without waiting for his response, she pivoted on her heel and slid out the door, careful to keep it tightly to her body, lest Max be seen.

Christ.

He wanted to be at her side, not her hidden shame. And he wanted to protect her, to keep Lady Fortune safe, to understand who was behind these attacks and why. To make certain they stopped.

Instead, he had pleasured her, and she had walked away. He did not like this feeling. Not at all.

CHAPTER 9

This time, the bastards had made off with silver, two paintings, and her damned ledgers. But they had also left a note.

It was the note which had been troubling Gen every bit as much as the latest invasion of her territory and subsequent thefts. Still sitting upon her desk, mocking her. One word. Misspelled, written in rude scrawl, but disturbing just the same.

Markwiss

"The sins of your fancy cull're going to be the end of Lady Fortune," Peter said harshly.

It was morning. Near dawn. Gen had spent the hours since learning about the thefts unable to sleep, plotting the means by which she would discover who was behind these attacks and destroy them. She was tired. Last night, the charleys had given her little hope that whoever was responsible would be caught.

And now Peter—and the note—were suggesting to her

that her problems were somehow related to the presence of the Marquess of Sundenbury.

Max.

She scowled at Peter. "He isn't mine."

But part of her wished he were, and that part of her was getting bigger and bolder with each day that passed. More dangerous, too.

"Could've fooled me," Peter said, lip curling. "When a cove's 'iding in a woman's room, usually means one thing."

It occurred to her that, somehow, she had allowed her relationship with Peter to grow too familiar. She was the leader here. She may have known him since she was a girl, and he may be taller than she and physically stronger, but it was not his place to comment upon her private actions.

Or any of her actions.

Hands clasped behind her back, she rounded her desk and stopped just short of Peter. The skull on his neck—one she had inked herself a few years ago—was a reminder of what she considered him to be. Another brother.

But her brothers would never confront her thus, and neither should he.

"I could have half London in my room if I wanted," she told him. "It's none of your concern whom I entertain."

His expression shifted, growing tense. "Never thought I'd see the day Gen Winter wanted to be a lord's ladybird."

"I ain't anyone's ladybird," she snapped. "Though if I were, I'd still be the owner of Lady Fortune, and you'd still work for me, and you'd still be venturing down a path you don't want to take, Peter."

She was warning him as best she knew how. She had never treated him as if he were anything less than her equal, but she was the leader of Lady Fortune. This roof and all that was left beneath it was her domain. Not his. And he had no right to question her decisions or integrity. Or to accuse her of being Max's ladybird.

She was no man's mistress, and she couldn't deny the insinuation stung.

Peter shook his head. "That the way of it now with us? You'll choose 'im over me?"

When Peter was angry, his accent became thicker; she'd worked hard to improve her speech, even if she had not always been able to quell her vulgar tongue. If the sudden darkness of his eyes was any indication, he was furious.

But once more, he had no right to be. "I ain't choosing anyone, nor should I. Sundenbury will be leaving us soon enough."

And why did something deep within her ache at the reminder?

"That note makes it clear as a windowpane why Lady Fortune's been attacked," Peter said. "Tell 'isnabs to go back where 'e belongs now. Before this gets worse."

Max had previously managed to amass significant debts with dangerous men, it was sure.

"The note means nothing," she countered. "And even if it does somehow relate to the marquess, that's my business, Peter. I'm the owner."

"But we're going to run it together." He reached for her, taking her hand in his. "You and me, Gen."

There was a new intensity in Peter's countenance. One she had never seen before. Or mayhap she had, but she'd always been too distracted to notice. It couldn't be that Peter had romantic feelings for her, could it?

"You're like another brother to me, Peter," she said quietly. "But I don't let my brothers dictate what I do, and I won't let you."

"And it's a brother's love I 'ave for you." His grip on her

hand tightened, and so did his jaw. "I want to protect you. Lords don't marry rookery rats like us."

Ladies had, she thought. Her brothers Dom and Devil had married Max's sisters, Lady Adele and Lady Evangeline. But it was true they weren't the duke's heirs. They were females; the line did not carry on with them.

She tugged her hand from Peter's grasp. "I ain't marrying anyone, least of all Sundenbury. I'm helping him, and he's helping me. That is all. Tit for tat."

Even as she made the claim, she recognized the lie in it herself. Things between them may have begun in that vein. But much had changed. She had never expected to desire him the way she did, with a desperation that was frightening as hell.

The door to her office opened, and the subject of their heated exchange sauntered over the threshold. Curse him if he didn't look ridiculously handsome for a man who had also been awake all hours of the night, attempting to help her restore order to Lady Fortune. Thanks to Max, Arthur had been discovered, locked in the larder, which had been blessedly untouched by the fire.

And Arthur was at his side now, happily trotting as if he hadn't a care in the world and as if the man whose side he attended were his true master.

Furred traitor.

"Forgive me," Max said, slowing his pace when his gaze took in the scene unfolding between Gen and Peter. "I did not intend to intrude."

No doubt he felt the tenseness in the air, hovering between Gen and Peter.

"And yet, 'ere you be," Peter snarled unkindly, "intruding just the same."

Arthur growled at Peter, taking Gen by surprise. He had always been quite friendly with the gentle giant.

"Arthur would like me to inform you he finds you terribly rude," Max said. "Hence the growl."

Peter took a step toward Max that Gen could only classify as menacing. He looked as if he wanted to trounce the marquess. She was sure Max could defend himself, but Arthur's subsequent bark and placement of himself between the marquess and Peter had her moving forward, slipping between the two men.

"Peter was just leaving. Weren't you, Peter?"

He glared. "I wasn't."

"Peter," she began, her tone one of warning, for she had not much patience left this morning.

"Look at that note," Peter interrupted, pointing toward the scrap which had been left. "Tell me you don't 'ave someone bearing down on you, someone you cheated, someone you owe. Everyone knows the Marquess of Sundenbury can't win a game to save 'is bleedin' life."

"I am aware of the note," Max said calmly. "I saw it last night, if you will recall. I remain just as perplexed by it now as I was then. I have not incurred a ha'penny of debt since my arrival here."

Peter snorted. "Cull's like you lie as soon as you open your mouth. Bad enough you're trying to make Gen into your ladybird. Now you're bringing your problems to 'er door as well."

Bloody hell.

Gen reacted before she could fully think, her fist connecting with Peter's shoulder. He was unsurprisingly solid for a man of his bulk. And damn it if the blow didn't make pain radiate from her knuckles, up her wrist.

"Enough!" she bit out. "Peter, if you don't get out of my office, you'll be hunting for a new job."

He jolted, as if she had slapped him. Somehow, her threat

had more effect upon him than the physical blow she had dealt.

"Fine then, if that's what you want." He rubbed his shoulder where she had punched him, his face inscrutable. "I'll go. But I'll be protecting you from the marquess 'owever I must."

With a final, pointed glare in Max's direction, Peter stalked from the room, slamming the door at his back. Arthur whined his displeasure. Gen stared at the closed portal, wondering what the hell had just happened.

"If I didn't know better, I would think I just walked in upon a lover's quarrel," Max said into the silence.

She turned to him, noting the dark circles beneath his eyes, the evidence he was as deprived of slumber as she. "Peter is like a brother to me."

Max raised a brow. "Mayhap someone ought to tell Peter that."

She just had. The marquess was deuced observant.

"Never thought I needed to tell him before," she admitted.

"He cares for you."

"I care for him, too. I've known him for years." Since before Gregory. Peter had been another child of the streets. "After Gav and I set out on our own, we banded together with a group of other lads. It was safer in numbers. Peter was one of them. That group was how we found Demon and realized we were family…"

She shuddered at the painful memories of that time, when she had been desperate for warmth and food, when they had picked pockets and shared their spoils to keep each other from the workhouse, or worse.

"Come," Max said, opening his arms to her.

For an embrace.

Part of her balked. Told her to run. She was strong enough on her own. She didn't need his comfort. Didn't want his sympathy. But the continued disasters at Lady Fortune had left her feeling closer to the scared urchin she had once been. And there was something undeniably appealing about being in the Marquess of Sundenbury's arms.

She went, wrapping her arms around his lean waist, pressing her cheek to the muscled strength of his chest. And his arms came around her as well, holding her tight, his warmth seeping into her. She had not realized she was cold until now. Nor had she realized just how much she wanted his comfort.

Arthur sidled nearer and sat on her booted foot, as was often his way when he was attempting to protect her. Max's heart was a steady, reassuring thump. His hands traveled up and down her back in soothing motions.

"I am sorry about what happened last night," he said, breaking the silence.

She tipped her head back, searching his face. "Sorry about what we did?"

His smile was wry. "Never that. Sorry about what we didn't do, yes. But sorry about the miscreants who seem hellbent on causing you mischief—I am sorry beyond words about that, Gen. I wish there was something I could do, some way I could find the bastards responsible and thrash them to within an inch of their lives."

Relief washed over her. She did not want him to regret what they had shared.

"None of what has happened is your fault," she said, though there was a small sliver of doubt which remained, persistent as a splinter.

"Do you believe that?" He searched her gaze, knowing too much, seeing too much, as always. "Your man seems to believe otherwise, thanks to our little note."

"I told him he hasn't a right to question you or what is between us."

His hands stilled in their caresses. "And what *is* between us, Gen?"

What a question to ask. She did not have the answer to it. At least, not the right answer. Not the one she wanted.

"We are friends," she said, lacking for a better descriptor, "are we not?"

He stiffened. "Like you and Peter are brother and sister?"

"No," she hastened to say. "It is different. It is...more. Much more."

His gaze plumbed hers, searching, seeking. "It hasn't escaped my notice that you didn't answer my question. The note, Gen. The thefts and destruction. They have only begun happening since my presence here."

Both his observations were true, and she could not deny it.

"The attacks on Lady Fortune have only begun following your presence here," she said. "I can't deny the note which was found, or what it says. Seemingly, there is a connection but I haven't an inkling what. I do not believe you are responsible, if that is what you are asking. Never."

"But neither do you believe me when I tell you I haven't any new debt?" he pressed. "When I tell you I have not played at the tables or made so much as a wager since the last, before I came here to you?"

Gen stared at him, wondering how she could answer. Struggling with her own turbulent emotions. She was tired and confused and on the edge of losing everything she had saved and worked for these last few years. Lady Fortune had been all she had wanted for as long as she could recall. But suddenly, it did not feel as if it were enough.

She wanted more. But she was afraid to trust anyone completely, outside of her family, and especially a man who had gambled his way through his privileged life. The Marquess of Sundenbury had never gone hungry, she was sure. He had never slept huddled with other urchins on the streets in the cold rain, trying in vain to keep warm. He had never had to worry about where his next meal would come from. Never had to fear what would happen if he were caught filching from some cove who'd wandered into the East End in search of vice.

He shook his head slowly, his expression turning mournful. "You don't believe me, do you?"

Did she?

Should she?

"I don't know what to believe," she confessed. "I want to believe you. But what has been happening here…and now the note. For weeks before your arrival, there was no trouble here. It seems an odd coincidence."

He released her, stepping back.

And she was bereft. Cold. All his heat and reassurance had been taken from her. The sole comfort which remained was Arthur, still planted upon her foot.

"If that is how you feel, mayhap it would be best if I go," he said quietly.

Coolly.

She hated the chill in his voice, in his eyes. Hated the absence of his dimples. Missed the teasing note in his voice, the comfort in his touch.

"Go?" she repeated, numb.

She was not prepared for such a reaction. Could not bear the thought of him leaving her. When their time together was at an end, yes. But she would have had time to prepare herself. More days. More hours. This was far too soon.

He nodded. "If you truly believe me an untrustworthy scoundrel who would imperil you, your future livelihood, and everyone in your employ, then why should I stay?"

When he phrased it thus, why indeed? She had no words. No explanation. Perhaps it was the lack of sleep or the shock of the latest havoc which had been unleashed, but her tongue felt thick, her mind sluggish.

"You should stay because we have a bargain," she managed at last. "One month of your time, a place for you to stay away from the trouble which has been dogging you, in exchange for your lessons. One month to find yourself back in your father the duke's good graces. One month to teach me how to be a lady."

"We did have a bargain. But conscienceless ne'er-do-wells do not keep their bargains, do they, my dear?" His voice was cutting as any blade. "So tell me, Miss Winter, which is it to be? Which man am I to you? Am I the man who would knowingly bring about the ruination of your business? Or am I the man you trust, the man you believe in?"

She hesitated. The decision was not an easy one. She had been wooed and charmed and duped before. Gregory had snuck into her room at the Devil's Spawn that long-ago day. She had been fifteen. He had been older, handsome, a man who praised her and kissed her and told her everything she wanted to hear. A man who had done so because he had wanted to force her brothers into taking him on as a partner of the gaming hell. A man who had another woman he loved, all whilst courting and seducing Gen. Thank heavens Gav had discovered what Gregory had been about before it was too late. Before she had given herself to him.

It was those memories which made her slow to find her answer. Those memories which had made her jaded and guarded. Which made her question trusting the man she had known the Marquess of Sundenbury to be before his arrival at Lady Fortune. One who gambled too much. Who could not answer his debts. Who had brought danger down upon not only himself, but his family as well.

She could not speak. Could not choose.

"I have my answer." Jaw clenched, the marquess gave her a

mocking bow. "Fear not, Miss Winter. I'll be gone in a quarter of an hour. You needn't fear I will bring any further trouble to your door."

"No," she said at last, for she did not want him to leave.

But it was too late.

He was already walking away.

She flinched as the door slammed for the second time. And then she sank to her rump on the floor and threw her arms around Arthur. He settled on her lap, licking her chin. But unlike so many other occasions before, his beloved presence did not soothe her. Because the Marquess of Sundenbury was going. And from this moment on, their paths would have scant few reasons to cross. His sisters were married to her brothers, but their social circles were worlds apart.

He was lost to her.

Lady Fortune would be too if she did not make it her sole concentration over the next sennight. She had advertised her opening day, and it was arriving soon. She had kitchens to repair, stolen goods to replace, and noblewomen to entice to her doors.

Damn it.

And damn the Marquess of Sundenbury, too.

CHAPTER 10

Max approached the rear door of The Sinner's Palace and knocked with more confidence it would open for him than he possessed. But he was a man on a mission, determined to seek an audience with Jasper Sutton himself. He had been haunted by his inability to help Gen ever since the day one week ago when he had packed his belongings and left her gaming hell behind.

Tonight, he'd had a sudden, sickening realization which had led him here.

Settling into the role of dutiful heir had not proven a pleasant task. Partly because Max was not, in fact, dutiful. But mostly because he missed Gen. He missed waking at Lady Fortune and seeking her out. Missed her bright-blue eyes and reluctant smiles. Missed taking her in his arms, missed her scent, her kiss, her touch.

Every damned thing about her.

That was what he missed.

He missed Arthur, too. The loyal hound had been an excellent companion, due, no doubt, to Max's discovery of his affinity for ear scratches. And the sausages he raided from the kitchens as bribery. But a man was allowed to have his secrets.

A slat in the door opened. A pair of eyes peeked at Max. They weren't particularly friendly eyes.

"Cove entrance at the front," the man snapped, then slammed the slat closed.

Max glanced down at his eveningwear. He was fresh from a ball his father had insisted he attend as a condition of being welcomed back into the familial fold. Fawning over marriageable ladies had been the object of the evening. Max had spent the entire night thinking of how he had taught Gen to dance. Wishing his every dancing partner were her. He had left the ball early, seizing upon the idea to seek out Sutton, without a care for how he was dressed or anything else.

His father would be enraged by his premature departure. Max did not give a damn.

He knocked on the portal again, this time with more force.

The entire portal opened, revealing a grim, dangerous-looking fellow. Not the same man who had offered Max and Gen entrance on their previous visit. This one was tall and broad, a hulking monster of a man.

"Told you," he snarled. "Wrong door."

"I am here to see Jasper Sutton," he announced, "and for that, I believe I am at the right door."

"He's occupied." The man moved to close the door.

Max wedged his boot on the threshold, preventing the movement. "Ask if he can spare a few minutes for Sundenbury."

"More coin to lose?" the man jeered.

So he was familiar after all.

"All the more reason to enter through the rear door," he said calmly. "No temptation."

It was true. Aside from the unused tables prepared for gaming in Lady Fortune, Max had deliberately kept his distance from the green baize. He missed the thrill gaming had provided him, and he was not naïve enough to believe he was completely inured to the lure. He had learned a great deal about himself during his time at Lady Fortune.

Unfortunately for him, one of the realizations was that he was in love with Genevieve Winter. A woman who was a law unto her own. A woman who distrusted him. A woman who could never truly be his.

"What d'you want with Jasper?" the man asked, seeming to relent now that he knew Max's identity. "He's with Henrietta and Maria, if you take my meaning. Won't likely emerge for another hour or so."

Henrietta and Maria? Max knew the names, not because he had been involved with either woman, but because he had seen them on the floor. The Sinner's Palace boasted some of the most beautiful ladybirds in the East End, and Henrietta and Maria were two of the loveliest. He supposed he should not be surprised Jasper Sutton bedded them himself, but two at once?

"I'll wait," he said.

The man shrugged. "If it pleases you."

"It is imperative that I speak with him tonight," he said.

Because tomorrow was the night Lady Fortune would open its doors for the first time, and he needed to be certain his suspicions were correct. If what he believed turned out to be true, Gen had a traitor in her trusted ranks.

* * *

"What do you think, Gen?"

She surveyed the hastily restored kitchens. The room still smelled of smoke, but the ash and destruction had been cleared away. Walls had been repaired. Furniture had been replaced. It was not perfect, but it would do.

She turned back to Peter, who was watching her expectantly. "Almost back to its old self. Thank you for overseeing all the repairs this past week."

Peter had been working day and night to undo the damage which had been done to Lady Fortune. And for the last sennight, there hadn't been any other incidents. It seemed as if the troubles which had been plaguing her had disappeared, along with the Marquess of Sundenbury.

Max.

She missed him. How she missed him. More than she was willing to admit. More than she had ever believed possible. But they had always been doomed to part, and his absence was for the best.

Peter nodded. "It's my duty. Least I can do to see Lady Fortune open 'er doors tomorrow as planned."

Tomorrow.

A shiver of anticipation cut through her at the reminder. The culmination of all her efforts. The word had been spread far and wide. A new, secret gaming hell for ladies. Reputations would be protected—all patrons would be masked. Even Gen herself would be masked as she made her way through the tables.

She could not deny, however, that her excitement was tempered by the sadness which had been her constant companion since Max had gone. She did not like this bloody inclination toward *feeling* he had created in her. Try as she might, she could not find a means of banishing it.

"I am thankful to you, Peter," she said softly.

Aside from the heated words they had exchanged concerning the marquess, her friendship with Peter had remained unshaken. She was especially grateful she had not needed to ask her brothers for aid. Lady Fortune, and all its problems, was hers. Solving them was her duty. Running it was, as well.

This place was in her blood and bones.

It was where she was meant to be, what she was intended to do, from birth. She wasn't a fine lady, never would be, and she'd do best to stop mooning over the memories of a handsome lord and his dimples and trudge on.

"I'm pleased to 'elp, Gen." Peter stepped forward.

He was crowding her. They were alone in the kitchens, which was not out of the ordinary, but he was standing near enough to her that the scent of him—the sharpness of male sweat—intruded.

She took a step back. "I should find Arthur and head for the land of nod."

Arthur had been spending each night guarding her faithfully. His presence comforted her and made her feel less lonely and vulnerable in the wake of Max's departure. Not that she would admit as much aloud to a soul.

"There's somethin' I'd like to talk to you about," Peter said. "We make a good team. I'll do anything for you and for Lady Fortune."

A knot formed in her belly. "Peter—"

"I want to marry you, Gen," he interrupted. Whatever 'appened between you and 'isnabs, I don't care. All I want is you."

"But..." Dismayed, she searched his intimidating countenance, hoping this was all a lark. "You said you think of me as a sister."

"It's more'n that. I love you."

The knot tightened. This was not what she wanted to hear. Or mayhap it was, but from the wrong man. Ruthlessly, she quashed all thoughts of the Marquess of Sundenbury. He was not here now, and nor would he likely be again. She had to accept that hard fact and look to her future.

A future that did not, no matter how fond she was of him, include becoming Peter's wife.

"You pay me a great honor, Peter," she said gently. "But you know I'll not marry any man. I'd never surrender my independence and everything I've worked for. Not for you. Not for anyone."

You would for one man, whispered a wicked voice inside her mind.

A voice she promptly dashed away.

"I wouldn't take anything from you," Peter countered, apparently unmoved by her polite refusal.

"You would, whether you wished it or not. The laws aren't on the side of women. I marry a man, and he owns my hell and me."

And that was the truth. Though, there was also the plain truth that she did not want to marry Peter. He didn't make sparks kindle into uncontrollable flames inside her the way the Marquess of Sundenbury did by merely walking into a room. She did not long for him, his touch, his scent. She had not spent the last week tossing about in her empty bed, wishing he were there. Wishing she had not sent him away.

One taste of passion with Max had not been enough.

It would never be enough.

"We needn't get leg-shackled then," Peter suggested. "I'll be your man. I'll be more man than 'is lordship could ever be."

Almost as if Peter's snarled insult had conjured him, a flurry of footfalls outside the kitchens heralded the arrival of intruders just before the Marquess of Sundenbury crossed the threshold, with Jasper Sutton behind him.

And they were not alone. There was a sullen stranger, wrists bound, face battered as if he had been at the mercy of some flying fists, at the end of Sutton's pistol.

"Gen," Max said, striding toward her.

Her name had never sounded so lovely as it did in his deep baritone and the crisp, clean accent she had come to adore. He was dressed bang up to the mark, looking as if he'd just walked from a ball into her kitchens. And mayhap he had. When he had been at Lady Fortune, he had dressed far more simply. Tonight, he looked every inch the nobleman and ducal heir he was.

Her heart clenched painfully in her chest.

"What are you doing here?" she asked him, hating herself for the way her voice emerged, for the longing hidden within its depths.

"Aye, what're you doing 'ere?" Peter demanded, positioning himself between Gen and Max as if he were her protector.

Gen didn't need a protector, and she didn't care for Peter's suddenly possessive air when it came to her. She sidestepped him.

"Odd you should ask," Max drawled, "as you are one of the primary reasons for my presence here."

"Me?" Peter scowled.

"You," Jasper Sutton said, nudging his captive with the barrels of his flintlock. "Tell Gen Winter what you told us, Wilmore."

Wilmore?

She took note of the man's split lip. "Ruben Wilmore?"

"Aye," he acknowledged, piercing her with a glare, though one of his eyes was swollen.

"Get that dirty dog out of 'ere," Peter spat, stalking forward with fists clenched.

"If there's any dirty dog here, it's you, Peter Moore," Wilmore charged.

Gen went cold, then hot with burgeoning outrage, then cold again as realization dawned on her. Ruben Wilmore was the man Sutton suspected of the attacks. And he knew Peter by name.

She turned to one of her oldest friends, and the sorrow she read in his face made her heart feel as if it had just been cast to the deepest depths of the sea. "Peter."

"He and Wilmore are behind the attacks on Lady Fortune," Max told her.

"That they are." Jasper Sutton delivered a particularly vicious jab to Wilmore's ribs that had the man grunting in pain. "Right amount of persuasion, and Wilmore here sang like a fucking bird. Didn't help he'd been running his mouth at The Sinner's Palace, telling everyone he could that he was getting his revenge on the Winters and earning pretty blunt for it, too."

"Your brother's the one what got mine killed," Wilmore shouted at her. "You deserve to suffer. All you bleedin' Winters do."

Betrayal was like a knife, cutting through her as she stared at Peter, a man she had trusted. "You went to him, didn't you?"

Peter hung his head. "I ain't proud of what I done, Gen. I know it was wrong, but when 'isnabs here started sniffing after you, I wanted to see 'im gone. I knew it was a matter of time before you was 'urt."

She shook her head, grief almost making her tongue immobile. "The way you hurt me, Peter? By setting fire to my kitchens, stealing my wine and my ledgers…"

It all made sense now. The letter implicating Max. The fact that Arthur had only caused a fuss the night of the fire when he'd smelled the smoke and that he'd been locked in the larder. She had never understood why her fiercely protective hound would not have barked at a trespasser.

But now she did. Because Arthur knew Peter, and because

Peter had made certain Arthur would be somewhere within the hell that he could not cause a disturbance.

"It weren't me what did those things, Gen," Peter said. "Wilmore did."

"Because you paid me to, you rotter," Wilmore countered.

"The charleys are waiting in the hall," Sutton said. "They'll be taking the both of you with them."

Charleys Sutton bribed, no doubt.

"You've done enough to her," Max told Peter. "Have mercy and go in peace."

But Peter's eyes were still on her, entreating.

"It makes me sick," she said. "To think of how thankful I was for all your help, cleaning up the mess you had made. None of this would have happened if not for you and your jealousy."

"I love you," he repeated. "I wanted to protect you."

"By destroying everything I have worked for?" She could not contain her laugh of disbelief at the daring in those words. "I don't want that sort of love, Peter. No woman would."

"Please—"

"No," she bit out, not wanting to hear another word, for there was no explanation he could offer which would induce her to forget what he had done. "I want you gone now."

Max seized Peter's arm. "Come, man. You heard Miss Winter. She doesn't want you here."

"You stay away from 'er," Peter growled, taking a swing at Max.

But the marquess was prepared, and he moved out of reach in time.

"Don't you dare touch him!" Gen cried, charging toward Peter, grasping the nearest available weapon that would harm without maiming.

A pot, as it happened.

She struck Peter on his beefy shoulder with as much force as she could manage. He yelped and turned toward her.

"Gen?" he asked, as if asking her forgiveness.

And she would give it to him. But not now. Not yet.

"Go." She shook her head. "Just go and do not come back."

* * *

At long last, the doors closed on the charleys, Jasper Sutton, and the two men responsible for the attacks on Lady Fortune. Gen faced Max, looking wearier than he had ever seen her. Sadder too.

His heart ached for her.

She had stormed to his rescue.

With a pot.

Max would forever hold the memory of his fierce empress attacking the massive brute who had betrayed her. She had dared to take on the wrath of a giant for him, and he could not lie. He had enjoyed watching her rush to his side.

Her defense was a week too late in coming, it was true. He could not deny that her lack of faith in him had hurt. *Hell*, it had hurt more than any physical blow he had ever received, and as he had been on the receiving end of more than one merciless thrashing over his unpaid debts, that was truly saying something.

He longed to take her in his arms, but he also recognized that much had changed between them on the day he had left. Further, that she was still grappling with the knowledge that a man she had considered another brother had been so treacherous.

She stopped just short of him, hugging her waist in a protective gesture he had never seen from her. There was such sadness in her eyes. Unlike most ladies in her circumstances, she was bereft of tears. But if there was anything he had learned in his time at Lady Fortune, it was that Gen Winter was not like any other woman.

She was herself, alone. An individual. Unapologetic. Determined. Stubborn.

Beautiful.

"I am sorry, empress," he said into the silence when she did not speak.

Her lips tightened. "What a silly thing to call me. I'm no one's empress. Least of all empress of this place. Couldn't even see what was plain as the beak on my face."

He moved nearer, closing the distance. Unable to help himself. The scent of her hovered on the air, and he felt inexplicably like he was coming home. Delicious, fragrant blossoms and Genevieve Winter. Was it her soap? He found it difficult to believe a woman such as she would trouble herself with perfume. Besides, he knew without doubt she smelled that sweetly *everywhere*.

"There is nothing about you that is plain," he told her softly.

She was wearing the same stricken expression which had been dominating her pretty features ever since she had discovered the truth about Peter. "That is where you're wrong, Marquess. Look at me. Then have a peek at yourself in the shiner."

She was speaking cant again, calling a looking glass a *shiner*. Gen was even more upset over this than she was allowing him to see. He knew her well enough to decipher her. At least, he thought he did.

He hoped he did.

He'd like to have the opportunity to know her even better.

Forever, whispered that voice in his head. The one he had been trying to ignore, the one that reached for more than he could have.

He gave in to the urge that would not be denied and touched her. Just a graze of his fingertips along her jaw. His hands were bare, and without a barrier between them, the heat of her seared him all the way to his elbow, and then beyond. There was an undeniable rightness. Her eyes widened, the blue deepening to the color of the sky at sunset.

"I do not need a looking glass to tell me you are the most glorious woman I have ever beheld," he told her earnestly. "And that neither I, nor anyone else, could hold a candle to you."

Polite society had a word for her. Incomparable. Gen Winter was the true meaning of that appellation, far more than any simpering debutante ever could be.

"I was wrong," she said, startling him with her admission. "Not just about Peter. About you. I am the one who should be sorry, Max. Not you. Never you."

It was more than he had expected of her. Far more.

He swallowed against a rush of emotion. "I should not have gone so easily. I should have seen what was happening. But it was not until I was at a bloody ball this evening, mid dance, that it hit me."

"You were at a ball?" Her query was wistful.

"Yes."

Now that he had started touching her, he could not stop. His fingers were on her throat, toying with the silken skin on display above her snowy cravat. Her pulse was racing. *Good.* She was not unaffected by him.

"Did you dance with the ladies?"

Her question took him by surprise. He answered her honestly. "I did."

But none of them were you.

He kept that bit to himself.

She nodded. "I don't suppose any of them stepped on your toes or tripped you."

God, how he loved this woman. The force of his emotion should frighten him, yet somehow, it did not. More fool, he.

"Not one." He tried to summon a smile, but even he knew it was a sad attempt at best. "Terribly uninspiring, the lot of them."

That won a laugh from her.

Hard-won laugh.

He wished he could capture it and keep it, place the mellifluous sound of her amusement in a box so that he might unleash it now and again over the years, when their lives took them far apart.

And then he wished their lives would never see them parted.

"You are as charming as ever, Blunderbury," she said teasingly.

He caressed her nape, that paradise where her skin was warm from the chignon there. "Back to Blunderbury, am I?"

He could not keep the regret from his voice.

Her levity fled. "It is better this way."

His head was dipping of its own accord, his lips hungering for the supple give of hers beneath them. "Better for whom?"

"Me," she whispered.

"Are we alone?" he asked.

"Arthur is in my office."

"The rest?"

She shook her head. "I sent them home. Tomorrow, if I have my way, we will be overrun. No need to work tonight when we sit empty."

A gift from the heavens, surely.

Still. He needed to make the choice hers. "If you send me away, I shall go."

His fingertips had found their way into her hair now, and he was gently massaging her scalp. There was such tension there. He longed to ease every bit of it away for her. To protect her. To kiss her. To make her his.

"Why would I send you anywhere?" She cast him a smile that on any other woman he would have supposed was an act of practiced flirtation. On Gen Winter, it was merely genuine.

Vulnerable in a way he had never seen her, not even when she had been naked before him.

"You were eager to be rid of me before." He found a knot and rubbed gently. "You work too hard, love."

She closed her eyes for a moment, leaning her head into his touch. "I was never eager to be rid of you. And I work as hard as I must. I was not born into wealth and privilege."

He had been. And he had never been ashamed of the circumstance of his birth. Indeed, before he had fallen in love with her, he had scarcely given a thought to his own advantage over others. It was merely what he had always known. But he saw it now, the inherent unfairness of this world. Understood it better than he could have had he not experienced his sojourn in the East End.

"Let me take care of you tonight," he said, then instantly regretted the words for the connotation.

He wanted to make love to her more than he wanted to take his next breath, and that was a matter of course. However, his desire to see to her welfare this evening was not carnal in nature. He wanted to ease her worries. To distract her. To tend to her when no one else was about to do so. Indeed, he suspected no man before him had ever done, and he aimed to rectify that travesty now. If she would allow it.

"You are a difficult man to deny, Marquess," she murmured, her voice throaty and low, eyes still closed.

"I have improved in your estimation in the last few minutes," he could not resist observing as he pressed a reverent kiss to her cheek. "I have gone from Blunderbury to Marquess."

He drew back in time enough to catch the fleeting smile on her mouth before it disappeared. "You charged to my rescue tonight, and I am grateful." Her eyes fluttered open then, her gaze bright and searching. "Tell me, why did you seek out Jasper Sutton? Why not one of my brothers instead? Or me?"

"I was not certain you would believe me. As for your brothers, I knew you did not wish to involve them in your problems, and that you wanted to solve them on your own. But I also needed someone with a good knowledge of the East End to aid me in finding the information I sought. Sutton seemed a reasonable enough choice since he was already familiar with Wilmore. I suspected Peter, but I also supposed he could not be acting alone. I needed proof, however."

"But you once owed Sutton a great deal of blunt. It is plain he is not an admirer of yours. Yet you sought him out."

She was not wrong. Gen Winter was an intelligent woman.

"I did it for you." Also truth.

"After I didn't believe in you."

He could not deny her words. Her lack of faith in him—along with his own pride—had driven him from Lady Fortune a sennight ago. And he had returned to the familial flock, dutiful. Reformed.

Miserable without her.

"I don't blame you for not believing in me," he admitted. "It hurt, I'll not lie. However, you have known Peter Moore for most of your life. You considered him like a brother to you. I cannot deny my past. I'm a ne'er-do-well who lost more money than he possessed at the gaming tables and drew others into his troubles. I would not trust me either."

"I do trust you."

Those three words, coming from a woman who had just discovered she had been betrayed by one man and who had hinted she had been similarly deceived by another, held a great deal of significance. But those three words coming from Genevieve Winter?

They meant *every bloody thing*.

He cupped her head, fingers trapped within the warm silk of her hair. "Does that mean I can stay here tonight, empress?"

She smiled. "It means you damned well better, Marquess. Or I shall punch you in the nose again."

She was teasing. He hoped. *Christ*, one never knew with her.

He grinned. "Anything but that. I promise to remain on one condition." He paused, thinking it over. "Nay. Make that two conditions."

She raised a brow. Her hands had come to rest on his shoulders, and she looped them around his neck now, using the action to tug his head lower. Bringing their mouths nearer. "Oh?"

"First that we check on Arthur together. It's been a week since I've been here to give him his meat scraps from the kitchens."

"Are you the reason that beast of mine has been haunting the kitchens?" she demanded.

He grinned, unrepentant. "Guilty. I've been giving him sausages. The little scamp loves them."

Her gaze sank to his mouth, and he swore she muttered something that sounded rather like *goddamn dimples*.

Max raised a brow. "I beg your pardon?"

She fluttered her lashes in an exaggerated imitation of a coquette. "I asked you what the other condition was."

Ha. She had not, and they both knew it, but he would play

along, because his other condition possessed far more potential for satisfaction than the first, his fondness for Gen's three-legged beast aside.

"My other condition is that you kiss me."

"With pleasure," she said, and then she rose on her toes, pressing her lips to his.

CHAPTER 11

Both Max's conditions had long been met. Kisses—accomplished. Arthur—safe in his bed. They walked into Gen's apartments, their hands linked, and he took a moment to observe it in a way he had not previously.

"You chose the wallcoverings?" he asked her.

They were yellow damask, cheerful. Not what he would have expected of the fierce, hardened woman he had initially come to know, it was true. But now that he had gotten the chance to see beneath her gruff exterior, the brightness made sense. It was how she was, like the sun in the sky after a vicious storm. Loveliness in the midst of darkness.

"Yes," she said, looking around along with him, a satisfied smile on the succulent fullness of her lips. "It is happy and hopeful when life so often is not."

Her life had not been, at least not when she had been a girl. Max knew it, and he hated what she had endured.

"It is beautiful," he said, his gaze clashing with hers. "*You* are beautiful."

"I am not." Rose tinged her cheekbones.

She had never been more glorious. Nor more vulnerable.

There was a difference to her this evening. All the walls had tumbled down, and she had no more artifice, no more bluster. She was only herself, as he had never seen her.

"You are," he pressed, because she needed to hear these words. Needed to know their truth. "You are the most beautiful woman I have ever known, not just for your exterior, but for who you are and what you do."

"What I do?"

"How hard you've worked on Lady Fortune, taking a pickpocket and a three-legged dog under your wing, everything."

"I inherited Davy from Dom, and Arthur found his way to me. He had been hit by a carriage. I nursed him. We could not save his leg, but he has never seemed to mind."

No, indeed. The hound was as effortlessly active as any Max had ever seen.

"You saved him," he said needlessly.

You saved me.

But he would not say that. Not now. Not yet. Even if it was true.

"Do not think me a saint," she said, voice low, eyes darkening. "Because I very much want to sin."

Yes. Oh hell yes.

"You are sure?" he asked, because he had to be certain.

She had told him he must stay or face grave peril to his nose. A sally, he knew. Her intentions had seemed clear. However, he wanted the decision to be hers. If she had misgivings, now was the time to embrace them.

"That I want to sin?" she asked, her arms looping around his neck. Unrepentant.

He clamped his hands on her waist, hidden beneath her gentleman's garb in the most egregious of travesties. But then, it also meant her body's secrets were his. "That you want me."

"Marquess." Her smile was wicked. Alluring, tempting. "I have never wanted another more."

"Thank Christ."

He did not wait. His mouth was on hers. Tongues met, dueled. Hunger for her was almost enough to consume him. Every part of him concentrated upon her, *Gen*. The connection of their lips. The need humming through him. She was everywhere. In his arms, on his lips, colliding with his most intimate thoughts, swirling through him, upending him utterly.

And that was before her hand settled on his cock.

But when it did…

He groaned into their kiss. She cupped him through his trousers, stroking his length with an ardor that, whilst untutored, was wholly delicious. And devastating. Enough to nearly bring him to his knees.

He tore his lips from hers. "If you continue with that, I'll not last long."

"With what?" she asked as she continued to torture him.

"You know what," he said, savoring this side of her.

It was bold and wicked. Heady and wild. Passionate and wanton and unlike anything he had ever known. Distinctively Genevieve Winter.

"This?" She stroked again.

His ballocks tightened. "Yes. *That*."

He could scarcely allow her to continue unchecked.

"I like touching you," she murmured.

He had unleashed a siren.

Max plucked her hand away with a mixture of reluctance and determination. "You may touch me all you like. But first, I want you naked."

"As the marquess pleases." Holding his stare boldly, she untied the knot in her cravat.

One flick of her fingers sent the linen sailing to the carpets.

She shrugged off her coat and set upon the buttons of her waistcoat.

Max's mouth went dry. The marquess was *much* pleased. He did not know if he could stand being more pleased. Every part of him was acutely aware of her. The scent, floral and sweet, the heat emanating from her, the vibrancy.

"I love your scent," he told her.

"Winters soap," she said, sending black silk to the floor before plucking the buttons at the neck of her shirt from their moorings. "One of the benefits of being a Winter, albeit a bastard one."

He frowned even as she whisked her shirt over her head. "I dislike that word, especially in conjunction with you. Cease calling yourself that."

"It is what I am." She faced him, unapologetic, clad in nothing but the binding she had wrapped around her breasts, and her trousers.

He trailed his finger down the center of the linen. "Why do you do this to yourself?"

"Keeps them from getting in the way." She smiled shyly and caught the lapels of his coat, tugging. "Off."

"It is a sin," he grumbled, but allowed her to help him shuck his coat first and his waistcoat next.

"It is practical. No one has ever complained before you, Marquess."

"As it should be." He caught the knot on her binding and undid it, beginning to unravel the linen. "If another man speaks of your breasts, I'll choke him with his own cravat."

Her smile deepened. "I like your bloodthirsty side."

She would. He rather liked hers, too.

The last of the binding fell to the floor. Her breasts sprang free, her nipples already hard. He lowered his head and sucked first one, then the other. Her fingers sifted through his hair, and she arched into him. He flicked his tongue over the stiff peaks, gratified when she moaned.

"One night," she said as he blew a stream of warm air over a straining tip. "That is all we can have."

One night? Fine time for her to decide to place limitations upon them.

He sucked hard on her nipple, then released it. "Why not more?"

She shook her head. "You know why."

He did, and he did not like it. Nor did he agree. But there would be time for that later, when his body was not raging with uncontrollable need for her. So he kissed the rosy nipples beckoning him and found the fall of her trousers.

She made a throaty sound of acquiescence and tore at his cravat and the short line of buttons on his shirt. Together, they pulled it over his head. Words fell away as they worked on the remnants of each other's attire. His need for her was so acute, so intense, and so, too, his love.

Naked, they slipped into her bed as one.

* * *

Finally.

That was all Gen could think as she lay on her bed and Max kissed her everywhere. Her body was singing, on fire, need pooling heavy and hot between her thighs. His mouth left flames and shivers in his wake, bringing her to life in places she had never imagined would desire to be kissed. Her shoulder, her inner elbow, her hip bone.

And then, his wicked hands were parting her thighs, and he had insinuated himself there, where the longing was making her wet and desperate for him. His head dipped. He tongued the bud of her sex. Her body jerked as if she were his marionette, being expertly played.

He was teasing her. Torturing her, really. Those light, swift licks making her press herself into his face with shameless abandon. His hands spread her wider, and then his thumb grazed her core, dipping into the place where she felt so empty. Where she wanted to be filled and taken.

By him.

Only him.

He raked her with his teeth, his thumb swirling, opening her, readying her. She was drenched and aching. He suckled her as if he wanted to consume every drop of her desire, and it was too much. The violence of her release took her by surprise. It was sudden and fast, quaking through her, sending the most exquisite pleasure blossoming from her center and radiating.

He kissed her inner thighs and then dragged his mouth upward, worshiping more of her body. Landing on her nipples. He made her feel...beautiful. Revered. It was, she thought, intoxicating. Already, she wanted more.

She never wanted this night to end.

"Gen," he whispered her name against her skin. "God, you are lovely." And then he kissed her scar, ugly and puckered. "So lovely."

She had no sensation where his lips grazed, but she felt those slow, tender kisses in her heart as he made his way along the length of that hideous reminder of what her mother had done.

Her fingertips dug into his shoulders. "I need you, Max."

There was no shame in the admission when she said it to him. Everything about them was different. She knew it.

He kissed over her breasts, taking his time, making her wild. His lips coasted along her neck as he settled between her thighs. The thick maleness of him had her moving, seeking more connection.

"Impatient." He kissed her ear, her jaw. "I am trying to take my time. I do not want to hurt you."

"I hurt now." She reached between them, her fingers closing around his length. He was hard and warm and soft. She stroked from root to tip, swirled her thumb over the round head, finding moisture there. "I ache for you."

He groaned and nuzzled her cheek, thrusting into her touch. "As do I, my love."

My love.

The endearment should have been unwelcome, and yet, it was not. She had always known the Marquess of Sundenbury was trouble. Here was more proof.

But she was helpless to resist that trouble. Or him.

"Please," she begged, all her pride gone.

He kissed her, slowly, languorously. The taste of her was on his tongue, foreign and musky. Strangely, she did not mind. There was an honesty in the carnality they shared. Everything about it, about him, felt *right*.

His fingers closed over hers, and together, they aligned themselves. He was at her entrance, and she was on fire. "Take me, empress. Take what you want."

She had a rudimentary knowledge of the way a man and woman fit together. Instinct prompted what that knowledge lacked. She guided him into her. They kissed again as he shifted, pumping his hips. And she was stretched and full, so gloriously full. There was a slight burning of discomfort as her body adjusted to the newness of his invasion.

She released her grasp on his shaft so he could thrust deeper. All the way inside. His fingers found the bud he had already tortured so deliciously, and he worked the sensitive flesh. Their tongues tangled as they kissed, and he withdrew, then pushed forward.

The rhythm was maddening. So too his touch on that part of her he had just pleasured. Each glide of his cock through her wetness was impossibly wondrous. She felt as if she were made of stars. As if she were sparkling and magnificent. As if she had been made solely for this pleasure, this moment.

This man.

The desire inside her was rising to a crescendo once more. As she moved with him, meeting him thrust for thrust, he flicked his thumb over her pearl. Again and again. Deeper. Harder. With one more stroke, he broke the kiss and drew hard on one of her nipples. She came apart.

Waves of bliss crashed over her. She shuddered and convulsed around him, and this time was more glorious than before, because he was inside her. A part of her. She clutched him to her, riding out the sensations until he suddenly withdrew. Grasping himself in his hand, he spent into the bedclothes at her side and then collapsed to the bed.

His arm slid around her waist, pulling her toward him. She went, nestling against the warm strength of his broad chest.

Savoring her marquess while she still could.

* * *

GEN WOKE LATE. So late, the sun was long risen over the East End. At least, that was what the weak light filtering in through the window dressing suggested. A masculine arm was thrown about her waist, a wicked lord's mouth was on her bare shoulder, and his hastily stiffening manhood was nestled against her bottom. Arthur, who had been fetched at some point in the evening following their second bout of lovemaking, was snoring blissfully at their feet.

For a moment, she allowed herself to lie perfectly still and revel in the wondrousness of the moment, the beautiful simplicity of it all. The head of the man she loved at her back, the innocent warmth of the companion she also loved at the end of the bed, the protective manner Max was curled about her, symbolic of the way he had been protecting and helping her from the moment he had first arrived at Lady Fortune.

Her chest felt full, her heart too big for its place in her breast.

There was something burning in her eyes.

She blinked as the room swam together, a mix of colors and light, shadows and indistinct shapes. She blinked some more, dismayed to find wetness on her cheeks, trickling down. Surely not…

Tears?

No.

She could count on one hand the number of times she had wept since the day her mother had sliced through her side with that merciless blade. The pain of her recovery afterward—the stitches, the infection she had barely survived—had not been enough to elicit such a response. One—that was the precise number, when she had stood in the burned remnants of Lady Fortune's kitchens. And yet, waking in her own bed with one man and one dog made her turn on the waterworks for the second time?

She sniffled, for her nose had now also begun to run. Gen had no wish to wake either man or beast. And she also had no desire to alert either to her maddening upset. Another moment or two, some deep breaths, a chance to shake off the chains of sleep which had likely addled her wits, and she would be fine.

But her deep breaths were shuddering. And more tears followed. Silent, stupid, weak tears. Slipping down her cheeks before she scrubbed them to oblivion with the back of her hand.

Because this morning would be their farewell.

After their charmed night together, there could not be another. He would return to Mayfair. She would stay here. He would one day marry. She would remain unwed. But this was the life she had chosen, she reminded herself. And she would have Arthur for comfort, her gaming hell to keep her busy.

It won't be enough.

The stark realization brought with it a fresh wave of tears, which could not be stifled no matter how hard she tried.

"Darling." He stirred, his hand gliding up and down her abdomen in a sensual caress that sent heat careening to all the places he had so thoroughly loved last night. "Why are you weeping? Are you in pain? I knew we should not have made love a second time—"

She turned to him and kissed him to shut him up. His instant response rewarded her. Their lips moved together, savoring, this meeting of mouths long and slow and lingering.

When she was satisfied she had distracted him from her humiliating tears, she broke the kiss. He cupped her face, his stare thorough, seeing far too much, she thought, in the early morning light.

"Your eyes are glistening, empress."

Empress. How she would miss being called that, as if she were someone important. As if she were someone special and elegant, a fine lady. As if she were *his*.

She blinked furiously at a fresh rush of tears. "I do not weep."

"You can be soft with me, you know." He kissed her cheek, her ear. "I like your softness."

And he showed her by caressing her breasts, her waist, her hips.

"You're charming me again, Marquess."

His lips found her throat. "Did you hear that?"

"What?" She was breathless now, and she was the one who was being diverted.

"The sound of your walls being erected once more." He nipped her lightly with his teeth as he cupped her bottom, his fingers tightening teasingly on her rump. "When I go back to Marquess, I know what it means."

He was not wrong.

"There is a dog in bed with us," she reminded him instead of responding to his statements. "I've no wish to play buttock ball with Arthur as audience."

Max's shoulders shook and she felt his smile against her neck. "Buttock ball? First time I heard that one, love."

She'd heard it from Demon, who had a love of finding new means of describing amorous congress, the more ridiculous the better.

Gen found herself smiling, for she loved this side of Max. "Could it be that *I've* taught *you* something new?"

He raised his head, the levity fading, dimples disappearing. "You've taught me a great deal more than that, Gen."

She wanted to ask what he meant, but she was afraid to hear the answer. So she kissed him again. "I'll miss you."

"Miss me?" He frowned. "I do not intend to stray far."

"Mayfair." She tried to sound unaffected and failed. Tried to smile and couldn't manage that either.

"Near enough."

Gen shook her head. "A world away."

"Gen," he began.

She pressed a finger to his lips. "Stubble it. We agreed to one night, Marquess. Don't ruin the time we have left."

He kissed her finger. "We can agree to more."

More would destroy her. The longer he lingered in her life, the more impossible it would be for her to give him up one day.

"We can't and you know it. We're too different."

His hands were traveling again, gliding along her waist. "In the best ways."

"In the wrong ways."

He kissed her, stealing her breath and her thoughts and her every objection for the moment. What could she do but open to his questing tongue, to kiss him back with all the fiery passion burning within? So she did. She kissed him and kissed him. As if these would be the last kisses they ever shared. Because they would be. They *had* to be.

He tore his mouth from hers at last to gaze at her with an expression of such adoration, she almost looked away. "Marry me."

Gen blinked. "Pardon?"

Surely she had misheard. Surely this was not the second proposal of marriage she had received in as many days. She, who had forever vowed she would never fall victim to the parson's mousetrap. She, who was in no way this man's social equal. She, who was not someone the next Duke of Linross could marry.

"Are you tap-hackled?" she blurted.

"No." He frowned. "And I can assure you, that is not the response I imagined I would receive when I offered to wed my future wife."

"Because I ain't your future wife." He was breaking her heart, the Marquess of Sundenbury. He was making her long for things she had no business longing for. Making her long for *him*, a future together.

Love, whispered an insidious voice. *Happiness.*

"I want you to be," he said.

Oh, Marquess. Only he could imagine a marriage between them would be possible when it was anything but.

"Wanting does not make something so." Her arms were

still around his neck, and she knew she should release him, but she was not ready to do so just yet.

"It does if one desires it badly enough." His countenance was earnest.

He was serious, bless him.

"Spoken like a man who has never been anything but a future duke with all the advantages of a lord." She tried to keep the bitterness away, but it was nigh impossible.

"Spoken like a man who loves you," he returned.

She froze. "You cannot—"

This time, he pressed a finger to her lips in an echo of her actions, staying her words. "Stubble it. I can. And I do. I love you, Gen. I don't want to marry anyone but you. Be my wife."

How she wished they were not naked, cocooned beneath the bedclothes, close as two people could be. It rendered her resistance that much more difficult. Necessary. But so damned hard.

She forced herself to pluck away his finger. "I'm a bastard. I own a gaming hell. I wear trousers. I can't dance. Hell, I can't speak properly. If you think the duke was furious over all the blunt you lost, how do you think he'd respond to a bastard Winter marrying his precious heir?"

"I do not care about any of those things. I will be the duke one day with or without my father's approval."

"So you say, until your fancy society turns their backs upon you because of me."

"My sisters are married to Winters and they have survived."

"Not unscathed, though. Doors have closed to them."

"Society can overlook a great many perceived faults for the right incentive. My sisters are finding their place," he insisted.

Wealth, he meant. And power. It was true that Dom had

become a powerful man, with many important men indebted to him.

But they were arguing and accomplishing nothing. Arthur shifted at their feet and let out a yawn.

She forced herself to be cold, to tamp down all her softness, and with it, the love, the hope, the foolishness. "You are thinking with your prick, Marquess."

"Is that what you intend to do?" he asked, recoiling. "You are going to turn what is between us into something vulgar?"

"It already is vulgar. I'm a bastard, and we aren't married."

"You are the woman I love, and I want to marry you. Don't do this, Gen. Don't turn your back on me. On us," he implored.

His heart was there, in his eyes, on his lips. He was offering it to her, surrendering everything. How she wished she could take it. But she could not. Later, he would thank her.

She disengaged from him and slid from the bed. "Morning is here. Time for you to return to Mayfair where you belong, Marquess."

CHAPTER 12

"Please tell me you have not returned to gambling," said Max's sister, Addy, the moment his arse hit the cushion of the gilded settee in her Mayfair salon.

What was it about all the females he loved having no bloody faith in him?

Max scowled. "I told you, I have cut loose the bonds of my past. I am a new man now."

And he had indeed felt like one that morning when he had awoken with the miracle of the woman he loved in his arms and her beloved hound at his feet. But that happiness had been hastily dashed by Gen's refusal of his offer for her. Now, he did not know whether to be furious or defeated or determined. After she had ordered him from her Lady Fortune, he had decided to settle for the latter.

Which was why he was here.

Addy had always been the shy, quiet wallflower to her twin sister Evie, and she had always been the twin to whom Max was closest, though he loved Evie equally. Still, it was the bond they shared which had brought Max here to Addy's home—though Evie lived next door with her husband, Devil Winter.

"You do not look like a new man," Addy observed, concern lining her countenance. "Forgive me, brother, but you look dreadful."

"There is good reason for that, and it has naught to do with gaming or losing funds," he said, before taking a deep breath and getting to the reason for his call. "It is because I have proposed marriage."

"Marriage?" Addy gaped. "When? And who is the fortunate lady? Pray do not say our father has forced you into offering for a lady who is not your choice."

He blinked. "This morning. The lady is your husband's sister, Miss Genevieve Winter, and she is the only choice I will ever have, our father be damned. I love her."

"You are wedding Gen?" his sister asked, as if the notion was akin to his announcing he was going to attempt to swim the length of the River Thames.

"The lady has refused my offer." His admission was reluctant and offered not without accompanying bitterness.

"Oh dear." If possible, Addy looked even more dismayed. "Did she give a reason for her refusal?"

"Something about her being born on the wrong side of the blanket, wearing trousers, and owning a gaming hell in the East End, I believe," he drawled.

"Yes." Addy winced. "There is all that."

"And I do not care about any of it." His hands clenched into impotent fists on his knees. "All I want is to marry the woman I love."

"Yet she has denied you."

He arched a brow. "Thank you for the reminder, unnecessary though it may be."

"What I meant by that observation is that she has reasons, reasons which she has given you for the rejection.

WINTER'S WALTZ

Reasons that are not irrational. You will be the Duke of Linross."

"I wish to God that it were not so," he bit out, meaning those words with every part of his being.

"You cannot change who you are," Addy said.

"No." He hung his head, raked his fingers through his hair. "I cannot. But surely there must be some way I can change the lady's mind."

He had been tormenting himself with the possibilities ever since he had left Lady Fortune. But every idea which came to him had a weakness that had proved its undoing.

"Have you told her you love her?" his sister asked gently.

"Of course I have."

"Have you said you are willing to take the risk of society turning a damning eye upon you and closing its doors?" she prodded.

"Yes, curse it all. And still, she has refused me."

"Have you asked her to cease operating her gaming hell?"

"No." Though now that he thought upon it, he did not recall directly relaying that to her. "She thinks there is no place for her in my world."

Her cutting words of earlier that morning returned to him. *If you think the duke was furious over all the blunt you lost, how do you think he'd respond to a bastard Winter marrying his precious heir?*

"It sounds as if she is trying to protect you," Addy said gently. "She is a fierce woman, and she would do anything to defend those she cares for."

"I do not need her to shield me from anything." Frustration ate at him. "I need her to be my wife."

"Then you know what you must do."

"Toss her into my carriage and run away with her?" he asked, unable to keep himself from an attempt at humor.

Addy shook her head, laughing. "Please do not do

anything that will leave my husband wanting to do you bodily harm."

Dominic Winter was a fierce opponent. A dangerous foe. Max had no intention of ruining the tentative pax he had with the man.

"Is that a no to abduction?" he asked wryly.

"Maximilian," she chastised. "That is a decided, vociferous no. But what you must do is *show* Gen why she should marry you."

"Have you the answer for how one goes about performing such a marvel?" he asked.

"Good of you to ask," his sister said, smiling. "I have an idea which I think may help you. However, Colin ought to be waking from his nap, and I must check on him first."

"Excellent. I shall hold my nephew while you enlighten me," he said.

"You are a good uncle, Max. And you shall make an even better husband."

Let us hope.

* * *

LADY FORTUNE HAD BEEN open for two hours, and already, it was thriving.

Gen was overseeing the success from the vantage point she had designed in her office. From her hidden window, she presided over a throng of masked ladies indulging in wine, cards, and dice below. Some of them appeared to be exchanging pleasantries, others laughing. All the work she had put into making certain news of her ladies' gaming hell spread throughout London appeared to have been rewarded.

The ladies had come.

In full force.

She had overcome all manner of adversities—treachery,

fire, and theft. She had worked hard, built a team of the best. Every part of Lady Fortune, from the carpets to the draperies to the paintings on the wall, was a reflection of her. She had chosen each detail. Before her was the proof of her success. So why, then, did her victory feel so hollow?

The answer was as troubling as it was clear: because Max was not here. Because she had sent him away. He had told her he loved her, asked her to marry him, and she had sent him off.

Mayhap she would never see him again.

A knock sounded on her office door. Likely, it was Davy, who had been removed from chamber pot duties in favor of being her right-hand this evening. With Peter gone, she had needed a substitute, and whilst the scamp couldn't be trusted not to pick pockets, he was as loyal as they came.

"Come," she called.

The door opened, followed by rustling and footfalls. Too many footfalls to belong to just Davy. She turned to find her half sisters—legitimate Winters and titled respectable ladies in their own rights, along with her sisters-in-law, Lady Evie and Lady Addy. Eight in all.

"I didn't expect any of you tonight," she said, bemused as the beautiful ladies, dressed in their finest evening gowns, filled her office.

Arthur, who had been dreaming in the corner on his favorite pillow, rose and barked before venturing to each lady and sniffing her skirts, as if to offer approval.

"We would not dream of missing the opening night of Lady Fortune." Lady Emilia Winter spoke first. She was married to Dev, the eldest of the legitimate branch of the Winter clan, and she was herself the daughter of a duke.

"You're not going on the floor, are you?" Gen asked, feeling slightly ill at the prospect of her half sisters and the wives of her brothers below, gambling and courting the potential for scandal.

"We will be masked." Her half sister Christabella grinned with glee. "This will be the most entertainment I've had since my confinement. Please do not attempt to dissuade me."

"Besides," her sister-in-law Addy said, "the most intriguing rumors are swirling about the owner of Lady Fortune. We must be there to witness it."

"A rumor?" Gen frowned. "But I've yet to go below. No one knows who owns Lady Fortune."

And she had kept it that way intentionally, in an effort to summon additional interest in her hell. An element of secrecy always appealed to everyone; she was sure lords and ladies were no different. But she would reveal herself soon enough.

"What if the owner of Lady Fortune were to remain a mystery?" asked her sister-in-law Evie, tilting her head as she considered Gen with a shrewd glance. "Do you not think it would add to the appeal of your establishment?"

"Whilst also allowing you to keep your involvement to yourself," suggested her half sister Bea.

"And enabling our matchmaking efforts to come to fruition," her half sister Eugie offered.

Pru, yet another half sister and the eldest of the legitimate female branch of Winters, smiled. "We were all pleased to hear the news."

News? Matchmaking? Gen felt suddenly as if her head had been filled with air, and that she was floating at the ceiling, like an ascension balloon attempting to make its way into the sky.

"What everyone is trying to say, with remarkable attempts at eloquence, is that you should marry Sundenbury. Keeping your identity as the owner of Lady Fortune a family secret will remove the chief impediment to your nuptials," said her half sister Grace, ever the forthright one.

Gen blinked, still trying to make sense of the sea of faces staring at her expectantly and all the information which had just been delivered. "Your matchmaking efforts, you say?"

"Max needed a second chance," Addy said softly, "and you needed love. From what I understand, you have both found that. All you need to do is seize it."

Her gaze narrowed. "Here now, listen to this, the lot of you. I don't like being manipulated, and I ain't about to marry anyone, least of all the marquess."

"There was no manipulation," said Lady Emilia, the picture of calm, lovely and feminine almost to a fault.

Two things Gen would never be.

"What do you call asking me to take on your troublesome brother?" Gen asked Addy.

Addy gave her a delicate shrug. "You did not have to accept."

No, she hadn't had to, had she? Nor had she been made to fall beneath the charming spell of the man and his dimples and his teaching her to waltz and winning over Arthur and kissing her so sweetly, and any of the hundreds of wondrous things he had said and done during his time at Lady Fortune.

No, curse them all.

Max had won her over well enough on his own. Sundenbury, she reminded herself.

"I won't marry him," she announced. "He will realize the terrible mistake I saved him from later."

"Love is never a terrible mistake," Evie countered.

"Who says I love him?" Gen grumbled.

Even though she did. She loved Max, the Marquess of Sundenbury, heir to the Duke of Linross, completely mismatched for her in every way.

Except for his kisses.

His touches.

The way he adored Arthur.

His laughter.

Those goddamn dimples…

"Your face does, darling," observed Christabella.

"Hell," she swore.

And then Max himself appeared on the threshold. Arthur trotted to him with a gleeful bound, as if they had not just seen each other that morning, as if it had been a century since they'd parted.

It felt like a bloody century. Being without him was terrible. Awful. How had she ever supposed she could manage it?

He gave Arthur a thorough ear scratch, but his gaze never wavered from Gen. "Empress."

"Well then," Lady Emilia said crisply. "I do believe the ladies and I shall head to the floor. I trust there shall be no scandals emerging from this evening?"

"None," Max confirmed, grinning.

Dimples, curse the man.

"Do not go," she said weakly.

But no one was paying her any heed. Her half sisters and sisters-in-law disappeared from her office one by one, until no one remained save the marquess and Arthur.

Both her loves.

Damn it. She would not turn on the waterworks again. She would not.

* * *

"You came back for me," Gen said softly.

Max had been hovering near the door with Arthur following the departure of the ladies Winter, uncertain of the welcome he would receive. But there was a vulnerability in her lovely countenance and in her voice that filled him with hope.

He started toward her. "I shall always come back for you. Chase me away as many times as you like, but it will not change my love for you. Nor, I hope, will it change yours for me."

She eyed him warily. He had not failed to note she was dressed this evening in the gown Madame Derosiers had given her. She was all ivory silk and sinful curves and utter perfection. He itched to touch her. To kiss her.

First, he had to convince her to marry him.

"Who said I love you, Marquess?" she demanded, chin tipping up, shoulders squaring as she emitted the same Genevieve Winter bravado he had come to know so well.

He stopped before her, their proximity intoxicating. "Do you not?"

She swallowed. Without the shield of her customary cravat, he spied the evidence of her discomfiture with ease.

"Sundenbury," she began.

"No Dunderhead?" he teased.

"No."

"Not even a Blunderbury?"

Her lips twitched. "Max."

"Better." His grin deepened.

"Bloody damned dimples."

This time, he had not misheard her. "What of them?"

"They make me mad," she admitted, glaring at him. "You're too handsome and charming."

He winked. "Tell me more, empress."

"And there you go again, calling me empress. You'll not find a lady much further from that lofty title than Genevieve Winter," she said.

He gave in to temptation then, tracing her jaw with the

backs of his fingers. Her skin was fashioned of silk and flame. "You are wrong, my love."

"Not the best way of persuading a woman to marry you, that," she observed, her voice taking on a husky tone. "Telling her she's wrong."

"I'll take my chances." He allowed his fingertips to trail down her throat. "Your tables are filled, Lady Fortune an undoubtable success. You are, just as Jasper Sutton said, the queen of the East End. Empress of all you rule: this gaming hell, me."

"Damn it, Marquess. You are making this far more difficult than it has to be."

Ever stubborn, his woman. Never mind. So could he be when the situation warranted it.

He caressed over her collarbone, his forefinger dipping into the hollow at the base of her throat. "No, love. You are making it far more difficult."

"What would you have me do?"

"Marry me."

"You'll regret it."

"Never," he vowed.

"You say that now, but how can I be sure?" Her eyes were troubled, searching his, seeking answers.

He took her hand, guided it to his heart. "This is how. My heart. It's yours, empress. It beats for you. Do you feel?"

Her lips parted. "Yes."

"I love you. I admire you. And I will continue to do so for the rest of our lives as long as you will allow it," he said, his voice shaking with the ferocity of his emotions. "I do not seek to keep you from being who you are, because that is the woman I fell in love with. You can continue to run Lady Fortune without my interference."

"Do you want me to keep it a secret, my involvement?" she asked. "As the ladies suggested I do?"

"Only if you wish it." That had been Addy's idea, a way of allowing Gen the freedom of continuing to live her life as she wished. "There will be sacrifices you must make as my wife, and I'll not lie about that. My father may not approve. He may cut me off. We may have to attend balls you find tedious, and you may have to occasionally don gowns such as this one."

She nodded. "You'll need to sacrifice too, Marquess. I have a vulgar tongue."

"I'd like to feel it on me."

She flushed. "I prefer to wear trousers."

"And I prefer removing them from you." His hand left hers to slide around her waist, pulling her flush to his body. "Any other sacrifices?"

"I won't give up Lady Fortune."

"I already told you I'd never ask it of you." Her curves were melting against him, and it took all the restraint he possessed to keep from kissing her.

"I'll always be a bastard born to the rookeries, most at home in the East End."

"I'll love you regardless of our geographical affiliations," he assured her.

"I'll love you, too," she said.

Shock and elation hit him at once, rather with the same force as a Genevieve Winter fist to the nose. "You love me?"

"Aye." She smiled, her sky-blue eyes glimmering with unshed tears. "I love you. And I'll marry you. I'll keep my identity a secret below. I'll do my best to protect you from scandal and shame."

Relief took the place of the shock, mingling with elation, and then another emotion. Sheer, unapologetic joy. He held her to him so tightly he feared he might crush her. "Do you mean it, Gen?"

"Yes." She frowned. "I'm cork-brained to agree, but…yes. I

love you, Max, and I do not want to be without you. You feel like a part of me. The *best* part of me."

He knew the sentiment. *Lord*, did he know it.

"Thank you." He lowered his head and claimed her lips.

The kiss was long, hard, and deep. Claiming, promising. It was a kiss of tongues and teeth, of possession and love and raw, beautiful emotion. They kissed until they were both breathless, and he rested his forehead against hers, their lips a feather's width apart.

"One condition, Marquess" she said.

He'd agree to anything at this point. As long as she would be his wife. "Yes."

"You don't know what it is yet."

"I do not need to." He kissed her again.

"No more sneaking Arthur treats from the kitchens," she said when at last their mouths parted once more. "That is the condition. All one has to say is *sausage*, and he howls like a Bedlamite."

As if to concur, Arthur barked.

"Sausage," he said, testing her assertion.

Arthur barked again, more loudly this time.

Gen raised a brow. "You see?"

He grinned. "I propose a compromise, for Arthur's sake."

"Dimples," she growled, and then she pulled his head back down, sealing his lips with hers.

EPILOGUE

A knock sounded on Gen's office door.

"Enter," she called, looking up from her ledgers.

Lady Fortune had been open for two months, and already, she had recouped her entire investment, earning a profit atop that. London's ladies were flocking to the novelty of an elite, anonymous gaming hell just for them. Best of all, her brother Demon had offered to take on the role of running the gaming floor. In the wake of her marriage to Max and her need for circumspection, it was the perfect balance. She was free to run her hell and to be with the man she loved, without fear of causing him scandal.

The portal opened and the same man she loved—her husband, the Marquess of Sundenbury, sauntered over the threshold, a basket slung on each arm. He was smiling, his dimples on full display, dressed to perfection, and handsome as sin.

"I come bearing gifts," he announced.

"I hope at least one of the gifts is something I can eat," she said, rising and crossing the chamber to reach him.

They had been married for one month, and they had

settled into a pleasant routine. They spent their mornings and evenings together, and her afternoons were at Lady Fortune, balancing ledgers, overseeing the replenishment of their various stores, learning from Demon what had happened the night before.

"Hungry, my love?" he asked.

Her stomach growled. She was ravenous. But now, her sudden hunger pangs had a reason. One she would tell him soon enough. When she gathered the courage and the moment seemed right.

"Always," she quipped, reaching for the basket nearest her. "Tell me you brought honey cakes."

"Patience, darling," he cautioned with mock severity, refusing to relinquish the basket.

A sound emerged from the wicker. One that sounded suspiciously canine.

Arthur rose from his bed and trotted forward, ears pointed and alert.

"What is in the basket?" she asked.

"One of my lady's gifts, of course."

Max was being his most charming.

But when wasn't he?

The last time he had been this charming, however...

"Have you been giving Arthur sausages again?" she demanded.

Arthur barked.

"You furred traitor," Max said to their beloved companion in mock outrage. "How dare you tell your mama that I have been giving you sausage? It was to be our secret."

Arthur cocked his head.

Gen compressed her lips to keep from smiling. "Is that the reason for the gifts? You are guilty, Marquess?"

"We are husband and wife. You may call me Max or husband, you know."

"Yes." She could not contain her grin. "I may. But needling you is great fun. Almost as much fun as two-handed put."

Her husband's cheeks turned pink. "Is that a new euphemism for lovemaking?"

"Aye." She grinned. "Not particularly new, however."

"Well." He cleared his throat, looking sweetly ruffled. "I, too, enjoy two-handed put. Along with making the beast with two backs. Or whatever it is you wish to call it."

She could not contain her laughter. "You'll do, Marquess. You'll do."

He raised a dark brow. "I'm relieved, love. We are wed, after all."

"That we are."

"Your gift, empress." He offered the first basket to her with a dramatic flourish.

She took it and flipped open the lid to reveal a puppy. He was black and white, his fur long, and he was missing an eye.

"Oh, Max. I love him." She pulled the pup from the basket and cradled him against her chest. He was warm and sweet and light as a feather. "Arthur, you shall have a brother."

Arthur sniffed the air, likely in search of a sausage rather than a sibling.

"Are you pleased? I know we have Arthur, but I found this little fellow in the streets without his mother, and I reasoned you are an excellent hand at rescuing all those who need it," Max said. "Myself included."

She was reasonably sure it was he who had rescued her, but he had just told her he had rescued a pup from the streets, and her heart was bursting. Or melting. Her eyes were most definitely watering.

Tears. She swallowed. Bit her lip. Heaved a sigh. But still, they remained.

"Thank you," she whispered.

"You have yet to see your second gift," he said, smiling at her in that way he had.

The one that made her feel so wonderfully loved. The one that made her feel as if she had finally found the one place in this world where she truly belonged—with this man.

"Honey cakes," he said, removing the linen covering from the second, smaller basket to reveal its contents.

Her stomach growled again, this time loud enough to echo in the room. "Perfect timing, my love. We are hungry."

She bit her lip after the revelation, wondering if he would take note.

But he was Max, so of course he did. He noticed everything.

The basket fell to the floor. "*We?*"

Gen took her time, lowering the pup to the carpets. Arthur sniffed him, and the two stared at each other. At last, she glanced back at her husband. "I am…we are…Arthur and New Pup are going to have another sibling. One with less fur, I should hope."

"We are having a child? You are increasing?" Max was grinning and his dimples were doing all the strange things they always did to her insides.

Oh, how was she to resist him? Thankfully, she did not need to.

"Aye, we are. I am." Hope and happiness blossomed inside her.

She had everything—the man who loved her, Lady Fortune, two dogs, and a child coming soon. What more could she ask for? The answer was obvious—nothing. Not one bloody thing.

Max took her in his arms, pulling her into a tight embrace as he pressed a reverent kiss to the top of her head. "I am so happy, my love. Happier than I ever thought I could be."

"As am I." Her arms were around his waist, her face buried in his chest.

"Kiss me?"

She tipped back her head. "Kiss me first."

And he did. And did. And *did*.

When at last they broke apart, their mouths were swollen and they were wearing matching smiles. By that time, Arthur and New Pup had eaten all the honey cakes. But neither Gen nor Max cared.

* * *

Dear Reader,

Thank you for reading Gen and Max's story! I hope you loved this eleventh book in my *The Wicked Winters* series as much as I loved writing their happily ever after!

Please consider leaving an honest review of *Winter's Waltz*. Reviews are greatly appreciated! If you'd like to keep up to date with my latest releases and series news, sign up for my newsletter here or follow me on Amazon or BookBub. Join my reader's group on Facebook for bonus content, early excerpts, giveaways, and more.

If you'd like a preview of *Winter's Widow*, Book Twelve in *The Wicked Winters* series, featuring Demon Winter and a proper widow seeking a second chance at happiness, do read on.

Until next time,

Scarlett

PREVIEW OF WINTER'S WIDOW

THE WICKED WINTERS BOOK 12

Demon Winter is an unabashed rogue. What better way to find more women to warm his bed than helping his sister Genevieve with her ladies' gaming establishment? It's the perfect arrangement. Until a duchess he can't resist walks through the doors and everything changes.

Mirabel, the widowed Duchess of Stanhope, has rigidly adhered to propriety her entire life, and all it garnered her was a miserable marriage to a cruel man. With her time of mourning over, she is on a mission to be wicked. Fortunately, the sinfully handsome, wildly unsuitable Demon Winter has offered to aid her in her quest. He's perfect for the task. Demon is a silver-tongued rakehell ten years her junior who was born in the rookeries. There is absolutely no chance Mirabel will fall in love with him. None.

A lady who has never broken the rules is about to break every one of them. But Demon Winter? He just may break her heart.

* * *

*C*hapter One

As had become a nightly ritual, Lady Fortune was brimming with London's wealthiest and finest females in search of diversion. Perfumed and powdered, masked and bang up to the mark in exquisite gowns, and all of them ready to wager their pin money or their husband's fortunes on the next turn of a card.

It was a beautiful sight to behold.

Demon Winter circled one of the faro tables at his sister Gen's exclusive ladies' gaming hell, on his way to the private room where a patron had requested to meet him. He was well accustomed to the lingering stares and longing looks the club members sent his way. But this—a demand to meet with him alone—was new. In truth, the lady in question—*number one hundred four*, by club records—had asked for the owner of Lady Fortune.

But as the bride to the Marquess of Sundenbury and a future duchess, Gen was keeping her identity as the owner of Lady Fortune a closely guarded secret. Which meant Demon would be meeting with *number one hundred four* instead of Gen. It was a nuisance he had not needed on a night that was already laden with problems.

The Madeira shipment was late.

Their resident scamp Davy had been caught filching a fan from *number two-and-twenty*.

Gen's new pup had shat in the kitchens, much to the outrage of their chef.

Demon sighed, then forced a smile in the direction of a brunette lovely who was attempting to catch his eye. At first, becoming the face of Gen's gaming hell had seemed a rum lark. Leave his position at The Devil's Spawn, a men's gaming hell, for an establishment overrun with ladies? Hardly a sacrifice.

However, there were nights like this one when Lady Fortune lost its bleeding luster.

Another few steps brought him to the door which led to Lady Fortune's private rooms, where its patrons could clandestinely engage in games with higher stakes. Or take dinner or tea. Whichever they preferred.

He reached the first private room, knocking before entering.

"Come," called an unfamiliar voice from within.

Number one hundred four was unknown to him. A relatively new patron.

Demon opened the portal, then crossed the threshold, closing it discreetly behind. Her back was to him, giving him a unique vantage point. In the low, intimate light of the room, her copper hair shone from its confinement in an elegant chignon. Her neck was creamy and elegant, enhanced by a golden necklace. Her shoulders were bare, making his gaze catch on one of his favorite places on a woman's body—that secret space where her neck and her shoulder met.

She turned, and his breath caught. For a moment, his annoyance fled. Even obscured though much of her countenance was by a gold, silken mask, she was beautiful.

"Sir."

"My lady." He bowed.

Demon Winter may have been born in the rookeries, but he knew what was expected from him by the quality.

She curtseyed, and it was then that he noticed the tremble —albeit slight—in her gloved hands. "Thank you for agreeing to an audience with me."

He nodded, wanting her to get the bloody hell on with it.

"Of course, my lady. It's my duty to make certain the members of Lady Fortune are well pleased."

Pink stole across her cheeks.

Fancy that, a lady who flushed. Interest flared despite himself. He had not intended those words the way she had interpreted them, but somehow, it no longer seemed to matter.

"So I have been told," she said, her blue gaze dropping to the floor, as if she were afraid to hold his stare for too long.

He found himself drawing nearer to her without realizing what he was about. She smelled bloody good, like something rare, floral, and exotic. He wondered where she applied the scent. Behind her ears? The hollow of her throat? Her inner wrist?

The possibilities were as endless as they were delicious.

Oh, what the hell was he thinking? He needed to rid himself of *number one hundred four* so he could make Davy clean up dog shit.

Demon stopped short of her. He knew his boundaries. "How can I help you, my lady? Say the word, and it shall be yours."

She wetted her lips with her tongue, then inhaled sharply. "I am in need of your assistance."

His assistance? The petticoats at Lady Fortune were an interesting blend of dedicated sinners and bored women in search of some means of entertainment. They had made all manner of requests thus far—hothouse pineapple, gin to supplement the Madeira, lewd publications, and the list went on. Never, however, had anyone asked him for assistance until now.

Demon could not deny he was intrigued. "I am listening."

She hesitated. "The matter is…a delicate one."

"What matter isn't?" he asked, impatience growing.

The evening had only just begun, and already, he had

tarried here too long, tempted by a lady he had no business being drawn to. Gen had made it clear as a window pane that the members of her establishment were not his for the tupping.

Her lips—a full, lush mouth, he noted, made for kissing—tightened in displeasure. "Indeed."

He was not telling her what she wished to hear. That much was apparent. But how was he to know what the devil she wanted? Standing there, looking so lovely, smelling so damned delicious. Tempting him.

Christ. He had no doubt Gen would tattoo his face in his sleep if he attempted to bed any of her fancy clientele. He had to force the woman to bloody well spill whatever it was she needed to tell him so he could carry on with the evening.

"What do you have need of, my lady?" he asked, impatient. "If it is a fruit or some such you're after, I will request it from the kitchens. If it's a game, I'll have it brought to the floor. If it's—"

"None of those things, sir," she interrupted, her body as stiff as an icicle hanging from the eaves, her voice just as cold.

"I ain't a soothsayer," he returned. "Before I can give you what you want, I need to know what it is you're after."

"This was an error on my behalf. Forgive me for importuning you." Her voice had softened, and he thought he detected a tremble in her chin. "I told Octavia coming here was a mistake."

The last, she muttered to herself.

The woman grew more fascinating by the moment.

"It's my pleasure to see to the happiness of all Lady Fortune's members," he said, trying for a bit of gallantry and thinking Gen would be proud. "Don't know who Octavia is, but I'm sure you being here isn't a mistake."

"Never mind who Octavia is." She caught her skirts in her

gloved hands and moved to swish past him, dudgeon high. "I was wrong to seek you out."

He should allow this mysterious, alluring woman to go. Let her disappear into the fabric of Lady Fortune, where the sea of masked ladies rendered each indistinguishable from the next. And yet, Demon caught her elbow as she made to pass him.

She stopped, turning toward him. Her eyes, the deepest shade of blue he had ever seen, cut straight to the heart of him.

He almost forgot himself, forgot it was *he* who had halted her. "I am here now, my lady. There is no need to run."

Her chin went up. "I am not running."

He dared to counter her. "Looks like you were trying to, doesn't it?"

What was the matter with him? He was not meant to defy the patrons. Gen would punch him in the eye if she knew.

Bloody good thing Gen didn't know. She was in Mayfair this evening. Far from the edge of the East End, this meeting of realms where London's elite came to play in decadence amongst the lords of the underworld.

"Secrecy is essential," she said.

The warmth of her was seeping into him, so he released her, disliking the effect she had upon him. How long had it been since he had last bedded a woman? Too long. He would have to rectify that. Soon, if the tightening of his trousers had anything to say about it.

"Upon my honor," he reassured the masked lady who had sought him out.

She didn't need to know he possessed scarcely any honor. He had what little his father had bestowed upon him. Curse Papa Winter to his lecherous soul.

Still, she hesitated, looking torn. "You do not know who I am?"

"Number one hundred four." His response was easy—that was all she was to him. All she could be.

Gen had developed an ingenious system for her membership, which had led to its rapid growth. The ladies were guaranteed their privacy. Each was assigned a number and nothing more. They entered Lady Fortune wearing masks and left wearing them. The ladies loved it—from the private gaming hell that was theirs alone, to the assurance their secrets were safe.

She rolled her lips inward, taking longer than necessary to answer him once more. And then, at last, she spoke.

"I require a lover."

Well, *hell.*

That was decidedly not what he had been expecting. At all. Also, would it be wrong to suggest himself for the position?

Demon could not stay the swift thought, but he promptly dashed it. Gen would kick him in the arse.

"Here now." He frowned. "I ain't a pimp."

Damn it—there went his efforts at speaking like a gentleman. He had been working on his unchecked tongue so well thus far.

"It was not my intention to suggest you were."

He stroked his jaw, considering her, enjoying her feminine curves in that gown far more than he ought. "Explain, madam."

"This club's attraction is its secrecy and circumspection."

Was it?

"Hmm. I thought it was the hazard tables," he said lightly, as if they were equals.

There was something about this moment between them that was personal. Intimate. *Carnal*, even. The very air seemed charged and ready to combust. Or mayhap that was just him.

Fuck. Was he flirting with her?

Aye. That he was.

And he had not an inkling as to her identity. She could be anyone. A lady, a mistress. *Hell*, she could even be a duchess. Not too goddamn likely, but the possibility remained.

"Hazard may appeal to some. Not to me, however," she said.

"Finding a man to bed you, however, does?" he asked, then cursed himself inwardly for the looseness of his tongue.

Gen would bludgeon him with the nearest available object for this, if she were to ever hear of it.

Number one hundred four pursed her lips. "You are being dismissive."

"Fancy words. All I do is run a gaming house."

"You are suggesting I should not wish for a lover," she elaborated, surprising him with her bravado.

The word *lover*, spoken in her dulcet tones, was making his cock hard. Her voice wasn't the only part of her having that particular, unwanted effect upon him, however.

He shook himself from the spell she'd cast upon him. "Men like me don't *suggest*. We say what we mean, and what I'm telling you is that Lady Fortune does not provide the kind of *circumspection* you're after."

"I understand." Her voice was cool, her demeanor icy. "Forgive me for my mistake."

She turned to go once more.

For some reason, a reason that emerged from deep inside him, murky and indistinct and yet forceful, he did not want her to go just yet.

"My lady."

She looked back to him.

"Mayhap I can be of help to you after all."

Want more? Get *Winter's Widow*!

DON'T MISS SCARLETT'S OTHER ROMANCES!

Complete Book List
HISTORICAL ROMANCE

Heart's Temptation
A Mad Passion (Book One)
Rebel Love (Book Two)
Reckless Need (Book Three)
Sweet Scandal (Book Four)
Restless Rake (Book Five)
Darling Duke (Book Six)
The Night Before Scandal (Book Seven)

Wicked Husbands
Her Errant Earl (Book One)
Her Lovestruck Lord (Book Two)
Her Reformed Rake (Book Three)
Her Deceptive Duke (Book Four)
Her Missing Marquess (Book Five)
Her Virtuous Viscount (Book Six)

DON'T MISS SCARLETT'S OTHER ROMANCES!

League of Dukes
Nobody's Duke (Book One)
Heartless Duke (Book Two)
Dangerous Duke (Book Three)
Shameless Duke (Book Four)
Scandalous Duke (Book Five)
Fearless Duke (Book Six)

Notorious Ladies of London
Lady Ruthless (Book One)
Lady Wallflower (Book Two)
Lady Reckless (Book Three)
Lady Wicked (Book Four)
Lady Lawless (Book Five)
Lady Brazen (Book 6)

Unexpected Lords
The Detective Duke (Book One)
The Playboy Peer (Book Two)

The Wicked Winters
Wicked in Winter (Book One)
Wedded in Winter (Book Two)
Wanton in Winter (Book Three)
Wishes in Winter (Book 3.5)
Willful in Winter (Book Four)
Wagered in Winter (Book Five)
Wild in Winter (Book Six)
Wooed in Winter (Book Seven)
Winter's Wallflower (Book Eight)
Winter's Woman (Book Nine)
Winter's Whispers (Book Ten)
Winter's Waltz (Book Eleven)
Winter's Widow (Book Twelve)

DON'T MISS SCARLETT'S OTHER ROMANCES!

Winter's Warrior (Book Thirteen)

The Sinful Suttons
Sutton's Spinster (Book One)
Sutton's Sins (Book Two)
Sutton's Surrender (Book Three)

Sins and Scoundrels
Duke of Depravity
Prince of Persuasion
Marquess of Mayhem
Sarah
Earl of Every Sin
Duke of Debauchery

Second Chance Manor
The Matchmaker and the Marquess by Scarlett Scott
The Angel and the Aristocrat *by Merry Farmer*
The Scholar and the Scot *by Caroline Lee*
The Venus and the Viscount by Scarlett Scott
The Buccaneer and the Bastard *by Merry Farmer*
The Doxy and the Duke *by Caroline Lee*

Stand-alone Novella
Lord of Pirates

CONTEMPORARY ROMANCE
Love's Second Chance
Reprieve (Book One)
Perfect Persuasion (Book Two)
Win My Love (Book Three)

Coastal Heat
Loved Up (Book One)

ABOUT THE AUTHOR

USA Today and Amazon bestselling author Scarlett Scott writes steamy Victorian and Regency romance with strong, intelligent heroines and sexy alpha heroes. She lives in Pennsylvania with her Canadian husband, adorable identical twins, and one TV-loving dog.

A self-professed literary junkie and nerd, she loves reading anything, but especially romance novels, poetry, and Middle English verse. Catch up with her on her website http://www.scarlettscottauthor.com/. Hearing from readers never fails to make her day.

Scarlett's complete book list and information about upcoming releases can be found at http://www.scarlettscottauthor.com/.

Connect with Scarlett! You can find her here:
 Join Scarlett Scott's reader's group on Facebook for early excerpts, giveaways, and a whole lot of fun!
 Sign up for her newsletter here.
 Follow Scarlett on Amazon
 Follow Scarlett on BookBub
 www.instagram.com/scarlettscottauthor/
 www.twitter.com/scarscoromance
 www.pinterest.com/scarlettscott
 www.facebook.com/AuthorScarlettScott

Printed in Dunstable, United Kingdom